The door crashed to the floor, landing on top of the screaming sentry

Bolan dived through the opening, firing the Desert Eagle as he moved. His comm unit was going crazy, with the FBI teams talking over each other. The four terrorists in the middle of the warehouse had armed themselves and were shooting wildly at the shadows around them.

Bolan ran for the only cover there was—a shadowed nook beneath the stairs leading to the catwalk. He took aim at the man closest to the bomb and dropped him with a well-placed round in the hip. The remaining terrorists didn't know where to focus their fire, and all three ran in opposite directions.

An FBI agent came through the broken doorway where Bolan had entered, and swiftly put two rounds into the chest of the man running toward him. That left two men on the floor and one on the catwalk.

Bolan scanned the metal walkway above him and spotted his target trying to pry open the window. The Executioner stealthily moved up the stairs, even as he heard the other two assailants go down in a hail of gunfire at the back of the building.

In his earpiece, the lead FBI agent said, "Stand down, everyone." Bolan ignored the command as he crept up behind the man frantically trying to escape through the too-small window. Bolan was just a few feet behind him when the man's senses must have told him someone was there.

The terrorist whipped around, pulling a 9 mm from his waistband. The Executioner gunned him down without hesitation, the echoes from his shot loud in the relative silence of the warehouse. "*Now* everyone can stand down."

MACK BOLAN ®
The Executioner

#330 Dual Action

#331 Assault Force

#332 Slaughter House

#333 Aftershock

#334 Jungle Justice

#335 Blood Vector

#336 Homeland Terror

#337 Tropic Blast

#338 Nuclear Reaction

#339 Deadly Contact

#340 Splinter Cell

#341 Rebel Force

#342 Double Play

#343 Border War

#344 Primal Law

#345 Orange Alert

#346 Vigilante Run

#347 Dragon's Den

#348 Carnage Code

#349 Firestorm

#350 Volatile Agent

#351 Hell Night

#352 Killing Trade

#353 Black Death Reprise

#354 Ambush Force

#355 Outback Assault

#356 Defense Breach

#357 Extreme Justice

#358 Blood Toll

#359 Desperate Passage

#360 Mission to Burma

#361 Final Resort

#362 Patriot Acts

#363 Face of Terror

#364 Hostile Odds

#365 Collision Course

#366 Pele's Fire

#367 Loose Cannon

#368 Crisis Nation

#369 Dangerous Tides

#370 Dark Alliance

#371 Fire Zone

#372 Lethal Compound

#373 Code of Honor

#374 System Corruption

#375 Salvador Strike

#376 Frontier Fury

#377 Desperate Cargo

#378 Death Run

#379 Deep Recon

#380 Silent Threat

#381 Killing Ground

#382 Threat Factor

#383 Raw Fury

#384 Cartel Clash

#385 Recovery Force

#386 Crucial Intercept

#387 Powder Burn

#388 Final Coup

#389 Deadly Command

#390 Toxic Terrain

#391 Enemy Agents

#392 Shadow Hunt

#393 Stand Down

#394 Trial by Fire

#395 Hazard Zone

#396 Fatal Combat

#397 Damage Radius

#398 Battle Cry

#399 Nuclear Storm

#400 Blind Justice

#401 Jungle Hunt

#402 Rebel Trade

#403 Line of Honor

#404 Final Judgment

#405 Lethal Diversion

The Executioner®

Don Pendleton's®

LETHAL DIVERSION

A GOLD EAGLE BOOK FROM

W✺RLDWIDE®

TORONTO • NEW YORK • LONDON
AMSTERDAM • PARIS • SYDNEY • HAMBURG
STOCKHOLM • ATHENS • TOKYO • MILAN
MADRID • WARSAW • BUDAPEST • AUCKLAND

First edition August 2012

ISBN-13: 978-0-373-64405-6

Special thanks and acknowledgment to
Dylan Garrett for his contribution to this work.

LETHAL DIVERSION

Printed in U.S.A.

'Tis now the very witching time of night,
When churchyards yawn and hell itself breathes out
Contagion to this world.

> —William Shakespeare
> (1564–1616)
> *Hamlet*

The devil isn't hiding in some dark corner of the universe. He is right here on earth, burrowing into the hearts of evil men, thriving on their heinous acts. The devil is all too real—and I am his greatest threat.

> —Mack Bolan

THE
MACK BOLAN
LEGEND

Nothing less than a war could have fashioned the destiny of the man called Mack Bolan. Bolan earned the Executioner title in the jungle hell of Vietnam.

But this soldier also wore another name—Sergeant Mercy. He was so tagged because of the compassion he showed to wounded comrades-in-arms and Vietnamese civilians.

Mack Bolan's second tour of duty ended prematurely when he was given emergency leave to return home and bury his family, victims of the Mob. Then he declared a one-man war against the Mafia.

He confronted the Families head-on from coast to coast, and soon a hope of victory began to appear. But Bolan had broken society's every rule. That same society started gunning for this elusive warrior—to no avail.

So Bolan was offered amnesty to work within the system against terrorism. This time, as an employee of Uncle Sam, Bolan became Colonel John Phoenix. With a command center at Stony Man Farm in Virginia, he and his new allies—Able Team and Phoenix Force—waged relentless war on a new adversary: the KGB.

But when his one true love, April Rose, died at the hands of the Soviet terror machine, Bolan severed all ties with Establishment authority.

Now, after a lengthy lone-wolf struggle and much soul-searching, the Executioner has agreed to enter an "arm's-length" alliance with his government once more, reserving the right to pursue personal missions in his Everlasting War.

"'Tis now the very witching time of night,
When churchyards yawn and hell itself breathes out
Contagion to this world."

—William Shakespeare

"'Tis the night—the night
Of the grave's delight,
And the warlocks are at their play;
Ye think that without
The wild winds shout,
But no, it is they—it is they."

—Arthur Cleveland Coxe

"From ghoulies and ghosties
And long-leggedy beasties
And things that go bump in the night,
Good Lord, deliver us!"

—Scottish saying

Prologue

The customized fifty-foot yacht sat low in the water of Lake St. Clair, rocking back and forth with the regularity of the low-tide waves. The full moon overhead lit up the craft and the smaller vessel attached to its side, floating together several miles offshore from Grosse Point Park, Michigan, in the border waters between Canada and the United States. A dispute here might be adjudicated by one country or even both, depending on who claimed jurisdiction and had the precise GPS coordinates to make such a claim. Malick Yasim expected that the location itself might add a certain tangle to the web that was being woven around the city of Detroit.

He skillfully climbed the rope ladder onto the sailboat, taking the lead ahead of his men. Stepping onto the deck, he flinched as a floodlight blinded him momentarily. *"Assalamu alaikum,"* he said, "now shut that damn thing off! It's bright enough to be seen from shore." His Afghani accent was barely noticeable.

The light went out, and was followed by a familiar voice. *"Wa alaikum assalaam.* I see that Sayid sent the Mummy himself to take delivery."

Yasim scowled at the nickname. Some called him that because they were certain his body count rivaled that of the mummies in Egypt, but Yusef liked to use it because at six foot two and bald as an egg, Malick's resemblance to the character in the movie was almost uncanny. There was little that he could do to dissuade the usage, but after this night he suspected others would make reference to it only in regard to his body count.

He waited for his eyes to adjust and for the three men he'd brought with him to come up the ladder. "Have you traveled all this way to mock me, or did you bring the merchandise Sayid requested? We have no time for foolishness."

Yusef stepped forward and shook Yasim's hand, kissing him on either cheek. "Do not be so temperamental, my brother. I have succeeded as promised. Come and see." In spite of the bulk he carried around his waist, the short man pivoted on his heels gracefully and headed below deck. Yasim followed close behind, watching the tassels on the man's red felt tarboosh swing to and fro.

The loss of the night air and the horizon line combined with the rocking of the boat caused Yasim's stomach to roll. It was the primary reason he hadn't been chosen to retrieve this merchandise from halfway around the world. He'd have never made it that long on board a ship and Sayid Rais Sayf believed that getting the uranium into the country was best accomplished by sea through Canada and into the United States.

To the naked eye, the main cabin of the yacht was nothing more remarkable than a well-furnished pleasure vessel, capable of long journeys. A kitchen, a galley, a table and benches that formed a U-shape in the corner. A short passage led to the sleeping quarters and a lavatory. Yusef walked to the table, unlocked the pins from underneath and revealed that it was actually a wooden top sitting on a large metal crate.

The container itself glowed faintly from the light of an electronic keypad on one side. Yasim moved forward, watching carefully as Yusef punched in a combination. The electronic locks popped open and he lifted the lid to reveal the long, slender rods of enriched uranium that he'd purchased for them in Iran. The box itself was refrigerated for safety, and the mist from inside floated around, giving an ethereal appearance to the deadly substance.

"You see, my friend? Everything is as I said it would be. There is nothing to cause you alarm." Yusef closed the container and punched in the code to lock down the lid.

"And the code?"

"Ah, the only six numbers I knew we would all remember. The years of our prophet's birth and death: five-seven-zero-six-three-two. Simple enough, yes?"

Trying to ignore the faint roiling in his guts, Yasim nodded. "Simple enough."

"Then, as I can see that you are already—what is the saying?—green around the gills, let us return to deck and finish our transaction. I am certain that Sayid must be anxious to have you safely back in port." He lowered the tabletop and replaced the pins. "Shall we?"

"There is one other matter that I must discuss with you first," Yasim said. "Privately."

"What is that?" Yusef asked, his eyes going a little white around the edges.

"While we were waiting for you to deliver the merchandise, word reached us that you spoke to the Libyans about selling them these rods instead of us."

Yusef sputtered, his face turning red before he finally answered. "I… *Astaghfirullah!* I will not insult you by lying, Malick, and I am truly sorry, but I am a businessman and I thought I might make a greater profit by selling the rods to one of my contacts in Libya."

Moving like a striking snake, Yasim whipped a thin-bladed knife from his belt, grabbed Yusef by the collar and forced him back against the bench. "It was *our* men who sacrificed to get you this cargo. *Our* blood that was spilled. *Our* money that was spent." He spat on the ground. "*Subhan'Allah!* If you were truly a believer you would not be seeking profit. You would give us the rods willingly, for our holy cause."

"Malick…you are right, I will ask for no profit. I will give this happily for the cause."

"You have no cause but yourself. Did you tell anyone else where you were delivering the rods? Or perhaps you told the rival who they were bidding against?"

"No! No, I swear. I only explored the option, but I knew that this is where Allah wanted the shipment to go."

"You should have known that all along." Yasim's blade sank into Yusef's throat, puncturing his larynx. The man thrashed and struggled beneath Yasim's grip briefly, but only briefly. He slumped to the floor and Malick offered a grim smile to the body. That would be the end of Yusef's whining and groveling. He was in Hell where he belonged, his passage to Heaven denied by his own traitorous actions.

He wiped his blade clean, then climbed back up on deck. The two crew members who served Yusef were dead on the deck. He nodded in satisfaction to his team. "Let us finish this work and get back on land. My stomach does not tolerate this well. If I never step foot on a boat again it will be too soon."

One of the men muttered a short prayer under his breath as they moved to unload the heavy crate from the yacht. Yasim prayed, too. He prayed that Allah would be with them as Sayid's plan was put in motion and that thousands of Americans would die because of his efforts.

This was their jihad, their struggle. Justice would be visited upon them for all the wrongs done to their people by the Americans.

1

Denny Seles, the Special Agent in Charge of the Detroit Field Office of the Federal Bureau of Investigation sat in his black SUV for a moment, watching the scene. He was pushing forty, and while he'd long since gotten used to the middle-of-the-night phone calls that were part of his job, they didn't usually come from the Coast Guard. More often than not, it was one of his field agents calling about a body. The flashing lights of an ambulance, along with two police cars, a fire truck and two other unmarked vehicles lit up the night. He flicked the Detroit Lions air freshener hanging from his rearview mirror, a superstitious habit he'd picked up along the way, and stepped out of the SUV.

Faintly, over the sound of voices and vehicles, he could hear the lapping of the waves of Lake St. Clair. He guessed that the large, white yacht grounded on the beach was the source of the call he'd received less than half an hour before.

"You must be Special Agent Seles?" a man said, stepping out of the crowd and extending a hand.

At six foot one, Denny wasn't considered small, but the man standing before him had him by a good three inches. He was tall and lanky, but offered a tired smile.

"Yeah, that's me," he said. "Special Agent in Charge, Denny Seles."

"Chief Richard Cline, sir," he said, and they shook hands.

"When the local guys told me your office had jurisdiction, your name and number were what they gave us. So you'll be taking over this mess?"

"If the local guys are right about jurisdiction, then yeah. Tell me what you got."

"A local fisherman called us in with a report of a boat run aground. We dispatched both a boat and a ground crew to the coordinates. Our ground crew got to the vessel first and backed out to wait for law enforcement as soon as they'd verified that everyone aboard was dead."

"You logged the caller's information?" Seles asked.

Cline nodded. "It will be in my written report, which will be on your desk by 0800."

"Good," Seles said. "Tell me what your ground crew found inside the boat."

"You've got three dead—two with bullet wounds to the head, one with a knife wound to the throat. But I think the important information, sir, is that this isn't an ordinary yacht."

His tone caught Seles's attention. "What do you mean?"

"I mean this isn't a lake cruiser. This ship has been modified to sail the high seas, complete with an extendable mast system and sails. She came from deeper waters than Lake St. Clair."

"A lot of ships in the Great Lakes are modified or even built to sail on the ocean. How do you know this one actually came from somewhere else?" the agent asked.

Cline chuckled. "I'm not guessing, sir. We ran the numbers on the hull. This boat was logged in the Mediterranean Sea three months ago and docked in Gibraltar around that time. All the permits for a non-commercial ocean crossing were found aboard."

"Interesting," he said. "You know anything else?"

"One last thing, sir. Beneath the table in the galley was a hidden, refrigerated compartment. It was empty, and when the local guys gave me the go-ahead on federal jurisdiction, I went ahead and ordered our forensic team to come in and do a full sweep."

"You suspect something more than drug-smuggling?" Seles asked. "Out here?"

"A refrigerated metal compartment, sir? For drugs?" The chief shook his head. "It doesn't add up."

Seles nodded, appreciating the man's professionalism. He hadn't dealt with the Coast Guard much, but every time he had, they'd been genuine pros. "Okay. Thanks, Chief. I think I'll go have a look-see."

The large yacht had come aground among the jagged rocks of the coast near Grosse Point, and it was canted awkwardly to one side. He was a bit skeptical about climbing up, but his hesitation was overcome as Chief Cline moved easily onto the sloped deck. Seles mimicked his steps and was soon on the slanting deck himself.

Two bodies were pressed against the rail and the polished wood was streaked with blood. The shots had been up close and personal, as the powder burns on their clothing were easily visible in the bright light being supplied to the scene by the Coast Guard. Staring at them, Seles could feel his stomach tightening. All of the anti-profiling training in the world didn't change his gut reaction after he'd spent two tours fighting in the Persian Gulf.

"I made sure our men didn't move the bodies," Cline was saying. "And we haven't let anyone else do much with the scene. Pissed the coroner off to no end that the locals were called, but I don't answer to county folks and I wasn't about to let them contaminate the scene. God knows how much damage our guys already did by accident."

"That's good work, Chief. Where's the third?"

"Down below deck," he said. "Follow me."

Seles's shoes slipped as they worked their way below deck.

He made his way down the steps and came up short as the container hidden beneath the galley table came into view. The heavy metal top lay open and the cooling lining looked like something out of a science-fiction movie. Denny immediately agreed with the chief's assessment and walked carefully into the room.

"How long before that team of yours gets here?"

"They're here now, sir," Cline said. "Shall I have them come aboard?"

"Do it," Seles said, then waited as Cline used his handheld radio to call them up.

A couple of minutes later, two men in hazmat suits walked on board, each carrying different types of detectors. The first team member who made his way into the cabin struggled with the lack of maneuverability of the suit in the confined space, and waved the second man back to the deck. Then he turned and stared at them wide-eyed. "What are your men doing in here without protective gear?"

"Hang on," Cline said, "before you get hazmat-crazy. We brought you in to look at this container to see if you could get any tracings off it. We weren't really expecting some major decontamination scene."

The man's eyes moved to the open container and then up to Cline's. "Your call, Chief," he said. Stepping forward, he ran his detector along the inside of the box, then pulled back and took off his helmet.

"It's your scene, Chief, but are you in charge of this mess?" he asked.

Cline shook his head and jabbed a thumb in Seles's direction. "That's your man," he said. "Special Agent Denny Seles, FBI."

"Makes sense." The man grunted. "Can I talk to you privately, sir?"

Seles could see the chief becoming flustered and getting ready to protest.

"What's your name?" the agent asked.

"Mike Kaminski, Petty Officer, First Class," he said.

"Okay, listen, Petty Officer. We've all been doing this a long time and your chief here was the one who had the foresight to get you guys en route before I even got here. Why the secrecy?"

The man straightened his spine. "No disrespect intended to the chief, sir. What he doesn't know, he can't talk about."

"Let's just have it," Seles said. "I've got my suspicions, but I want confirmation and that's where you come in."

"All right," Kaminski said. "That's a lead-shielded, refrigerated container. Very recently, it held uranium."

"Can you tell what kind?" Seles asked.

"Weapons-grade variety," he said. "And from the looks of the container, I'd say you're dealing with a substantial amount."

"Give me an estimate," Seles said.

"Easily twenty-five kilograms or more would fit inside that container, especially in rod or brick form."

Seles sighed and nodded. "Okay, gentlemen. No one outside this room talks about this or gets this information until I say so. Understood?"

Both men nodded at once. "Chief Cline, I want your ground team to set up a hard perimeter, and no one—that includes local law enforcement—gets through. Tell them…" He paused as he considered and discarded several stories, then settled on one. "Tell them there's a minor chemical spill of some kind in here and until we get it cleaned up, no one's allowed aboard."

"We can handle that," Cline said.

"Good," Seles replied. "I'm going to have some teams in here shortly and they'll go over this boat, the bodies, everything, with a fine-toothed comb. No one touches anything else."

"We got it," Cline said.

"I'll be back in a few," Seles said, "but I've got to go make some calls." He worked his way back out to the deck, down to the rocks, and from there to his SUV. Once he was inside, he pulled a number up on his list and almost laughed. He'd never thought to call it in a million years. He dialed, waited and a moment later a woman's voice answered.

"Office of the Director," she said. "This is Melinda Harris speaking."

"This is Special Agent in Charge Denny Seles, Detroit," he said. "I need to speak to Director Wallace, please."

"He's in a meeting, sir," she said. "I can have him call you."

"Interrupt him," he said.

"Sir, he's in an important meeting and—"

"Miss, this is a national-security issue. Put me through right now."

She paused for a moment, then said, "Hold please."

Seles waited on the line for Wallace's voice, which he knew from phone conversations and the rare meeting in person.

"Seles, what the hell could be happening in Detroit that is so important that you pull me out of a meeting with the… never mind. What's so pressing?"

"I've got a national security matter," he said. "It's serious."

"In Detroit?" Wallace asked, sounding incredulous. "What the hell's going on?"

"Someone, somewhere near here, has weapons-grade uranium. We just found the boat they used to bring it in."

Wallace was quiet for a moment, then Seles clearly heard him say, "Melinda, clear my schedule and get me the White House on the other line."

HAL BROGNOLA SAT in his hot tub simultaneously trying to position his kinked back in front of the jets and keep his cigar stub out of the water. He never smoked cigars, but he enjoyed chewing on them, and his taste in them was far too expensive to lose one in the water. As the Project Director for Stony Man Farm he could arrange for strike teams, clear up a terror threat and avert international disasters, but the day-in, day-out tension would make any man long for a massage. He'd have to settle for hot-water pressure jets, and as he relaxed, it began to work its magic on his sore muscles. He closed his eyes, sighing in relief.

He dismissed the first ring of his cell phone as a dream. It had to be. The second ring, however, reminded him that wanting something to be a dream often clashed with reality. Only a handful of people in the world had his number. He pushed himself out of the hot tub and reached for his phone, noting that the call was from a secure, blocked line.

"Hal Brognola," he said.

"Hal, this is the President."

Brognola felt his tension return with a sudden vengeance. "Mr. President, sir."

"Hal, there's a situation in Detroit," the President said. "It could be very serious."

"Go ahead, sir," Brognola said.

"The Coast Guard found a boat run aground in Lake St. Clair. Three dead men and a container that had recently housed uranium. Hal…we have weapons-grade radioactive material on U.S. soil."

"How can we help, Mr. President?"

"All the usual organizations are already doing their song and dance. They've activated the Detroit Emergency Operations Center and all the field agencies are coordinating through them."

"That sounds right," Brognola said. "Do you foresee a problem of some kind, sir?"

"I wish we had foreseen any of this. That's the problem."

"We can only react to what's in front of us, Mr. President."

"All right, Hal, here's the deal. All our normal agencies are going to be up to their eyeballs in protocol and their little fiefdoms and covering their own asses. I've already had the Directors of the NSA and the FBI in here, shouting at each other about whose fault it was. In the meantime, before they get it all together, these terrorists could blow up Detroit. I want you to send someone in to cut through all the red-tape bullshit. If he runs into any snags with the locals, tell him to have them authorize through the Office of the President. I want this found and handled."

Brognola knew that sometimes fate put the right man in the right place at *just* the right time. "As it happens, Mr. President, I have a man in the area already who will be perfect for the job."

"Then get him working, Hal. We don't know what we're up against or how long we've got until these bastards do whatever it is they plan to do."

"I'll contact him immediately, Mr. President," Brognola said, hanging up with a polite goodbye.

The man for the job was Mack Bolan. And if there was anyone who could hunt down and stop bad guys, it was Striker. The man sometimes called the Executioner.

2

The Military Demarcation Line—the line that divided North and South Korea—was as real as the line 8 Mile Road represented to the residents of Detroit. The road marked the barrier between black and white, rich and poor. It was a boundary in some ways, and in others, it was a no-man's-land where only the strong survived. The Executioner watched the street below through the cracked glass of his window.

His room was on the second floor of the 8 Pine Motel, an establishment that let rooms by the hour, day, week or even month, depending on how long a person could pay. Most paid by the day or week, depending on whether their income was from drugs or prostitution. The johns paid by the hour, and the elderly, living on a fixed income and a bit wiser than the others, paid by the month. None of them were particularly happy, but Bolan couldn't blame them. The 8 Pine Motel was not a happy place.

Sadly, it was representative of many of the buildings on this stretch of road. Cracked, broken or boarded-up windows, peeling paint, gang graffiti, bad water from lead pipes, and everywhere the smell of fear and desperation. Bolan's room was little more than a mildew-scented mattress with a broken frame, a scarred bedside table and a bathroom where the only thing that ran were the cockroaches. He'd stayed in worse places, but most of them had been in other countries that were either impoverished or at war. It was little wonder that the major drug smugglers had decided that Detroit was a target-rich environment.

He'd been in the city for the past two weeks, cultivating information about the now-booming heroin trade that had found its focus here. On the street below him, he watched as a car stopped and the man driving bought some crack and then drove on, while the dealer stepped back to his wall to wait for the next customer. There was little concern about the police in this area—they didn't want to come near it unless they had to, and when they did, they came in force, giving the street dealers all the time they needed to disappear.

The next customer turned out to be a kid about thirteen. Bolan watched as the girl obviously begged for more. The dealer stood his ground. He stepped forward and began to grope the girl and then nodded toward the alleyway.

Bolan slipped out of his room and into the alley just in time to hear a smack resounding off brick walls.

"I thought I could, I can't, but I'll get you the money. I just need…"

Another slap rent the air and Bolan stepped out of the shadows as the dealer raised his hand high in the air again.

"I don't think you want to do that."

The dealer turned just enough to see Bolan, but kept his quarry on the ground in front of him. Tears spilled from the dark-ringed eyes of a girl who was growing up way too hard, way too fast. She tried to move, but he pushed her back down.

"Get the fuck out of here, man. Don't be messin' around in my business."

"Normally, I wouldn't, but you picked the wrong target today and the wrong corner to stand on."

The dealer pulled a gun from the waistband of his pants and pointed it at Bolan as he swaggered down the alleyway.

"Look, bitch, this is my alley and my street and that bitch

there, yeah…she's going to be mine, too. Now if you don't want me to leave you bleedin' here, you'll turn your ass around and get the fuck outta here."

The dealer moved closer, confident in the gun he was swinging around in his hand. Bolan was patient until he was just in range. He grabbed the gun and yanked the dealer forward as he brought his knee into the man's ribcage. Bolan heard the satisfying sound of the ribs cracking and then brought his elbow around to break the dealer's nose.

Blood spurted as the man dropped to the ground and cried. Bolan was surprised that he didn't just yell, but actually lay in the alley, crying. He picked up the gun and went to check on the girl who'd remained motionless during the confrontation.

"You could have been shot, why'd you do that?"

"Because everyone deserves a second chance. You got parents?"

She nodded. "My dad, but he's never home."

"Look, I'm going to make a call. There's a rehab center close to here, it's inpatient and this guy owes me a favor. Will you go?"

"I can't pay."

"I didn't ask if you could pay, will you go?"

"Why?"

"Because everyone deserves a second chance."

BACK IN HIS ROOM, Bolan stood, and stared out the window at the corner where the girl had gotten in trouble. Turned out her name was Violet and she'd really needed the help. He'd made sure the dealer was picked up and put away and couldn't blow his cover and then sat back and enjoyed his mediocre cup of coffee and contemplated his next move.

So far, all his leads had been toward the Muslim community and some kind of pipeline out of Afghanistan. His cover was flimsy, but holding so far: he was representing a buyer from Los Angeles who trusted his muscle more than the information he'd received so far. The process of building trust, however, and getting close to the source, had proven tedious at best.

In fact, without some new leads, Bolan was going to have to try to get his information in a more direct way. The biggest challenge was a simple one: he was a Caucasian from the United States trying to convince a group of Muslims from the Middle East that he was trustworthy. It wasn't going well.

These were the thoughts running through his head when his cell phone rang. He pulled it from his belt and recognized the number on the display as a secure call sign. "Bolan," he said, answering it.

"Striker, it's Hal," the reply came. "We've got a situation."

"Don't we always?" he asked.

Brognola chuckled, but he had to force it out.

"Okay, so it's a serious situation," Bolan intimated. "What's going on?"

"Have you made any progress on your investigation in Detroit?" he asked.

Stepping back from the window, he took a seat on the bed. "Not very much," he admitted. "It's slow going. Why?"

"I'd like you to change focus. This is more pressing than any pipeline heroin and comes straight from the White House."

Bolan could almost hear his old friend chewing his cigar stub to shreds. "Fill me in," he said.

"There's a potential nuclear threat inside the city," Brognola said. He quickly filled him in on the boat found by the Coast Guard, along with the results of their sweep, and Denny Seles's quick response so far.

"That works out pretty well," Bolan said. "I did a passing-through hello with him when I got here. So he's already got my DEA credentials and we got along well enough. What's the status of local law enforcement?"

"Right now, they just got their Emergency Operations Center up and running. There's a woman in charge there, Allison Hart, but Denny will take the lead on field operations. You've got White House clearance to do whatever needs to be done to find the uranium rods and stop whoever is behind it."

"I'm game, Hal," Bolan said, "but it sounds like they're doing all the right things."

"They are," he agreed, "but you and I—and the President—all know that over the next few hours, every federal law agency in the country is going to start fucking around with protocol this and red tape that. The President wants a man there who can cut through all that and just get the job done."

"And he doesn't think Seles is that man?"

"He's the Special Agent in Charge of the Detroit Field Office, so he's going to be by the book from beginning to end. I've read his file and he's a good man, but he's not you. We need you on this one, Striker."

"All right, Hal," he said. "I'll close up shop here and head over to the EOC and see what I can stir up. Do they have any leads?"

"Nothing concrete yet."

"A target? A threat? Anything?"

"We've got three dead guys on a yacht in Lake St. Clair and some missing weapons-grade uranium. I'll shoot the file to your handheld via a secure uplink. The rest is up to you," Brognola replied. He laughed drily. "Situation enough for you?"

"Sounds like it," Bolan said. "I'm on my way. I'll check in with you when I know more." He disconnected the call and put the phone back on his belt, his mind considering the possibilities. A moment later, the file came through and he looked it over. The dead men were all Middle Eastern. Not much more information than that.

Before he went to see Denny Seles, there was another man who might be able to help, even if it blew his cover. Weapons-grade uranium took precedence, and right at this moment, he needed information more than anything else.

Bolan quickly packed up his few things, making a quick sweep to ensure that the room was empty of his belongings. Slinging his bag over one shoulder, he slipped out of the room and down the hall to the stairs. If he moved fast enough, he might be able to talk to the man he needed to see before his evening prayers.

THE ISLAMIC TEMPLE OF TRUTH was a combination mosque and community center at what Bolan had come to think of as ground zero of the 8 Mile region. Over the past couple of weeks, he'd come to believe that the man who ran it, Imam Aalim Al-Qadir, genuinely cared about the Muslim community and he'd been willing to share information so long as it didn't lead to more trouble for anyone.

The imam was in his mid-forties, with skin the color of a French-roast coffee bean and a white goatee and mustache that few men could pull off, but the imam somehow did. Bolan had never seen him in anything other than traditional Muslim garb, complete with a dark red tarboosh that sported golden tassels. He wore silver-framed glasses and a smile that could disarm the angriest members of his mosque.

Bolan pulled his car—a nondescript sedan that had already come close to being stolen several times—into a parking space in the back of the building. Al-Qadir had been forthcoming about his concerns in regards to the 8IM gang, and he'd shared them with Bolan. He had to hope that the man's contacts in the community would help with something far more pressing and important than the illicit activities of the 8IM gang.

He locked the car and went to the back door, where he rang the bell and waited. From experience, he knew that there was a camera positioned on the roof of the hall beyond the door, and that the imam would be checking his video feed before he answered. It was only a minute or two wait before Al-Qadir appeared, unlocking the door and greeting him warmly in the traditional fashion. "*Assalamu alaikum,* my friend," he said.

"*Wa alaikum assalaam,*" Bolan replied. "It is good to see you. Can we talk in your office?"

Al-Qadir nodded pleasantly and led the way, offering tea once they'd reached the small space. It was a small rectangle, perhaps ten by fourteen, with a large metal desk that looked as though it came straight out of a 1960s school, several bookcases, and many pictures of the Muslim children in the community on the walls.

Bolan turned the tea down with a shake of his head, and took a seat across from the imam.

"Your face is serious, Matt," he said, using the name Bolan had given. "What troubles you?"

"You have been honest with me," he said, "and we've had a good dialogue. I think we've come to know each other a little bit. I am troubled because of news I received today and that my original intentions here have to change."

"Go on," Al-Qadir said, sipping his tea. "I sense your hesitation, Matt, but I cannot help you or our community without information."

Bolan nodded. "As I told you when we met, I work for the DEA. But often, I hear about things from other federal law-enforcement agencies. A short time ago, I heard from someone at the FBI. A ship was found in Lake St. Clair with three dead men aboard—all of them from the Middle East. They found evidence that weapons-grade uranium—the kind

used to make nuclear weapons—was on board the ship, too."
He watched the man's face carefully as he shared these last
words, but all he saw was shock and sadness.

"This…this cannot be related to anyone I know, Matt," he
said. "Many of the young people here are in gangs and involved with drugs. I would be foolish to deny it. But no one
has said anything about acts of terrorism!"

"I believe you," Bolan assured him. "But *someone* in the
Muslim or the Islamic community knows, Aalim. Someone
knows something. I need your help."

The imam sat quietly for several long seconds, considering his words, then he sighed and nodded. "What do you
want me to do?"

"I need you to start asking questions, pressing people a
little just to see if you get a reaction of any kind. We don't
know who's behind this, but I think it would be safe to assume that whoever it is has a lot of money, and, in this neighborhood, that means drugs and possibly prostitution. Even if
they haven't done anything themselves, someone may have
heard something."

"In my experience, Matt, extremists in this country do
their best to stay quiet," the imam said, shaking his head.
"Unless I happen to stumble upon the person who is actually involved, it is unlikely that someone will have heard
something."

Bolan shook his head. "Maybe, but something like this
takes a lot of planning, a lot of men. Please, Aalim."

"I will do what I can. Do you believe that 8IM is involved?"

Bolan shrugged. "I don't know," he admitted. "It's possible
and it's a place to start, but it could be anyone."

"And if I find something out, I should call you at the number you gave me?" he asked.

"Yes, as soon as possible," he said. "Thank you."

"You're welcome, Matt. The Holy Koran teaches peace,

not violence, and we cannot allow extremists to take root among us. It will only make becoming part of the American culture more difficult."

Bolan thought for a moment, then said, "There's one more thing, Aalim. Be careful. Don't ask too many direct questions. If whoever is behind this hears you asking questions, they'll kill you. I have no doubts about that."

"My eyes are open, Matt," he said, rising to his feet. "And now I sense you wish to leave?"

Bolan got to his feet. "Unfortunately. There's a lot to do and I have to move quickly. Call me if you hear anything at all."

"I will," Al-Qadir said, offering his hand, which Bolan gladly shook. "Stay safe, my friend."

"You do the same," he replied. "I'll show myself out."

"Fi Amanullah," he said.

Bolan nodded and headed back down the short hallway. He had a feeling he'd need more than Allah's protection if the situation escalated, and in his experience, a fully loaded Desert Eagle was more reliable than a god in a fight anyway.

Still, he thought as he headed back to his car, any blessing was better than none at all.

3

The Detroit Emergency Operations Center was housed downtown, in a nondescript office building two blocks from the Wayne County Courthouse, and in the largest law-enforcement precinct in the city. When Bolan arrived parking was already at a premium, which meant he had quite a walk. On the other hand, the walk gave him plenty of time to observe that every branch of law enforcement, as well as fire, medical and emergency-management personnel were already present. It was a regular house party.

He was stopped at the main entrance, but flashed his DEA credentials and got to the reception desk, where a harried-looking security guard was manning the phones. "Can I help you, sir?" he asked.

"Matt Cooper, DEA," he said. "I'm looking for Denny Seles."

The guard looked at his credentials again, and nodded. "He's in the main communications room, giving a briefing. If you want to catch him, that's the best place to look. Down the left hallway. You can't miss it."

"Busy here today," Bolan observed.

The phone beeped insistently, and the guard shrugged. "You don't know the half of it."

"I wouldn't bet on that," Bolan replied, heading down the hall. The guard had been right about one thing—it would be impossible to miss the communications room since the hall led directly to it. The room was set up a bit like an auditorium, though there was no stage, but instead a bank of screens lit up one entire wall. Denny Seles was standing at a portable podium, and behind him on the screens, various potential target locations were being displayed as he discussed where law-enforcement personnel were going to be stationed. In front of him, tiered rows of computer stations looked down, and in addition to the people seated at them, the room was filled almost to overflowing with people standing around. At the top of the room was a set of offices, the largest belonging to the Director of the EOC.

Seles finished up his briefing and answered a few questions, then dismissed everyone. He stayed down front, talking to a small group of people, including a woman Bolan assumed was Allison Hart, the EOC Director, according to the file Brognola had sent him. She was strikingly beautiful and obviously of mixed Asian descent. Her expression at the moment was serious, but Bolan could see the smile lines around her mouth and eyes.

When it looked as if the group was ready to break up, he worked his way down the auditorium to where Seles and Hart were still talking. Seles must have spotted him because he stopped talking and signaled for him to come over. Bolan did so, offering a hand when he got closer.

"Special Agent in Charge Denny Seles," Bolan said. "We meet again."

"Special Agent Matt Cooper," the agent said. "I thought you were undercover over in the 8 Mile region." He paused, then introduced Bolan to the woman. "Allison Hart, Special Agent Cooper is with the DEA. He came by as a courtesy when he arrived in town a few weeks ago."

"It's nice to meet you," she said. They shook hands.

"What can I do for you, Matt?" Seles asked without preamble. "As you can see, we're kind of busy today."

"So I hear," Bolan replied. "I was briefed a short time ago. I thought I should drop in and offer my help."

Denny's lips pursed as he considered this information. "You're an undercover DEA agent and you were *briefed?*" he asked. "By whom?"

"Someone higher up in the food chain," Bolan said, shrugging. "They thought your mission was more important than mine, so here I am."

"Look, Matt, if we've got a leak here…" he began.

Bolan held up his hands. "No, there's no leak."

"Then I've got to know where you're getting your information from," Seles said, his voice regretfully firm. "I can't do this if every federal law-enforcement agency in the country is going to come in here without telling me."

Bolan thought about it, and then said, "Look, Denny, I'm something of a specialist. I came here on an operation for the DEA, but my orders today are coming from the White House. Call and get confirmation from the West Wing."

Hart laughed lightly. "You were ordered here by the White House?" she asked. "Give me a break."

Bolan stared at her, capturing her eyes with his own blue gaze. "Make the call, Miss Hart," he said. "We're wasting time arguing about where my orders came from instead of being out there catching the terrorists."

She nodded once. "I will," she said, then turned and headed for her office.

"You're on the level, aren't you?" Seles asked.

"Yeah," Bolan said. "So where do you want me?"

"Allison is going to head up the EOC, and I'll be in charge of field operations. The best thing you could do for me is pound the streets. Use the informants you've got to see if you can dig up something, anything. And maybe take another look at the boat. I might have missed something."

Bolan nodded. "I can do that. I'll stop by there first. What have you got so far?"

Seles sighed heavily. "As of right now, not a damn thing."

"No threats, no intelligence chatter, nothing?" he asked.

"Not even a hint," he replied. "I'm posting people at high-value targets, and my field team is ready to move on a moment's notice, but until we get some hard intel, we're just staging."

"What's your gut tell you?"

"That we're in deep shit," Seles said. "We just don't know how deep yet."

"Waist-high and rising fast," Bolan said. He gave the special agent a business card with his cell number on it. "I'm heading out. Call that number if you need me. I've got yours already."

"That come from the White House, too?" Seles asked, half-jokingly.

"Nah. It was on your business card when we met," Bolan said. He turned and headed back up the risers toward the exit. He saw Hart in her office, a phone pressed to her ear and offered her a grin and a salute as he left.

She'd better get focused on the important things, Bolan thought, because he had a feeling that they were already way behind the terrorists, and weren't catching up anytime soon.

HIS REAL NAME WAS Sayid Rais Sayf. That was the name given to him by his parents when he was born in Afghanistan and it was the name that he prayed to Allah with for guidance. But few people in Detroit knew this name—very few, and only those who could be trusted to die without speaking it. Everyone else knew him as Michael Jonas, age forty-two, a successful man who had worked his way out of a tough life, growing up adopted, and was presently at the peak of his career.

As he parked his Audi A8 in the jammed parking lot of the Detroit EOC, he mentally became Michael Jonas. While he was here, he would think as Michael Jonas, react as Michael Jonas, he would *be* Michael Jonas in all respects, because everything he had worked for could unravel like a spool of thread should any trace of Sayid Rais Sayf show in his face, mannerisms, speech or actions. His car was just one part of the costume he wore, no different than his tailored suit, his salon-styled hair or his accent-free speech.

Coming to the EOC on this day was a risk, he knew, but a small one. His girlfriend, Allison Hart, had agreed to dinner later and he had come by to give her an opportunity to cancel in person. While he must feign ignorance, his true purpose in dealing with her was the same as it had always been: information. Information was power, and because he knew more than they did, he had power over them. As he would even when the bomb went off.

Sayf checked his suit one last time in the mirror; it was a charcoal-gray pinstripe worn with a dark blue tie. Then he stepped out of the car, locking it behind him. It was unseasonably warm for Detroit in late fall, but he wore a long jacket nonetheless. He wasn't a particularly big man, but he carried an imposing presence in his five-foot-eight, 185-pound frame—and the long coat was a part of that. People saw what they wanted to see.

He walked quickly to the entrance, and saw that he wouldn't even get past the door without identification, which he casually provided. The policemen at the entrance instructed him to go inside and stop at the security desk. Jonas nodded pleasantly to them both, then went inside. The man at the desk was familiar to him, and he smiled in greeting.

"Officer Robards," he said. "What's going on here today?"

"It's crazy," he said, reaching for the phone on the desk. "Hang on and I'll let Allison know you're here."

"I can't go back?" he asked. "Is there a problem?"

Robards shook his head. "No one but law enforcement is getting back there today, I'm afraid. Like I said, crazy."

Sayf affected a shrug. "I'll wait," he said, putting his hands behind his back and walking in a slow circle in the lobby. He hadn't expected to get into the EOC, but it would have been a nice bonus. As it was, he would have to see how much he could pry from Hart.

It took her nearly ten minutes to come out to the lobby, but she greeted him with a kiss on the cheek. "Michael," she said. "I'm sorry to have kept you waiting."

"It's no problem," he said. "Is everything okay?"

She shook her head. "Unfortunately, no. We've had to stand up the EOC. I'm afraid I have to cancel our plans for this evening."

"You must be joking," he said. "We have dinner reservations at Opus One tonight!"

"I wish I were," she said.

"There is…trouble?" he asked. "I didn't hear anything on the news and the weatherman said the skies would be clear."

"Let me walk you to your car," she said, taking him by the arm. "I'll explain as much as I can on the way."

He allowed her to lead him back out of the building and into the parking lot. "You seem very upset, Allison," he said. He already knew that the boat had been discovered and he was quite angry with Malick Yasim, but he would deal with him later. For the moment, he needed to play the solicitous boyfriend.

"I am," she said. "There's a…threat to the city. A terrorist threat. Until we can lock it down, I need to stay at the EOC to coordinate our response." She looked up at him and he was struck again by her physical beauty. She was a very spiritual woman, but she was not Muslim. Like the car or the suit, she was simply part of his disguise.

"I see," he said. "So it is serious. Should I be worried? What kind of threat?"

She shrugged delicately, then peered around the parking area for his car and started in that direction once she saw it. "We don't know, at this point, who's involved or what their plan is, but the threat seems serious enough. I can't tell you much more, just that the threat is radiological—and I shouldn't even say that."

"My God!" he said, pretending surprise. "And you don't have any idea of what their actual plan is?"

She shook her head. "No. That's what we're working on now."

"Perhaps we should cancel the game tomorrow night," he suggested. His job as the head of Security for Ford Field—the home of the Detroit Lions—provided both income and a very high-profile cover for his work. "This kind of danger. So many people. It's Halloween and we're expecting a full house."

They stopped at his car and she leaned into him. "Michael, no one can know. Don't cancel the game yet. That would just start people asking questions and sooner or later, a panic. I'm sure we'll get it figured out before then."

"I hope so," he said. "I'll call the restaurant and cancel our reservations. And I won't say anything, but you must promise to keep me informed."

"As much as I can," she said, kissing him on the cheek. "I've got to get back, but I'll call you later, okay?"

"Of course," he said, returning the kiss. His disgust at the public display of affection didn't show on his face. He unlocked his car and got in. "Call if you need anything. Would it be all right if I increased security at the stadium?"

Hart nodded. "Just do it quietly."

"I will," he said. He started the engine, then drove away, quite satisfied. They knew very little and Hart was obviously very afraid. He could see it in her posture, her eyes, and hear it in her voice. Fear was a powerful weapon, too, and those who were scared didn't make good decisions. It would serve his purposes quite well.

4

The flashing blue and red lights from various law-enforcement vehicles were nearly blinding as Bolan pulled to a stop and parked his car. He wanted a look at the boat, but he'd expected the area to have calmed down by this time. The notion that they were going to keep this situation under wraps was going to be pure fantasy if they didn't scale things back quite a bit. He left his vehicle and flashed his DEA badge at the two county sheriff's deputies that stood guard in front of the path down to the beach where the yacht had beached. They motioned him to pass on through without stopping him.

He'd reached the rocky shore, noting the three body bags on the ground, and was contemplating whether to check the boat or the bodies first, when he was stopped by a tall, lanky man in a Coast Guard Chief's uniform. "Excuse me, sir. Can I help you?"

There was an open honesty to the man's face that Bolan liked to see in law enforcement. "You must be Chief Cline. I'm Agent Matt Cooper. DEA. Denny Seles sent me your way," he said.

Chief Cline shook his hand and then a quick flash of recognition followed. "That's right. I got a text from Seles that he might be sending over another set of eyes. What can I do to lend you a hand?"

"Well, the first thing you can do is send about seventy-five percent of these people home or back to their regular patrol. And tell the others to turn off their emergency lights. All this is drawing way too much attention to the scene. I don't know why Seles didn't mention it before, except he's a man with a lot on his mind."

Cline looked around, taking in the sight. Bolan knew that when someone was in the middle of something, it was hard to see it from the outside.

"You're right," he said. "There are too many people here for a simple boat-run-aground scenario. I'll start clearing them out immediately. What else?"

"Have you learned anything new since Seles was here earlier?" he asked.

The chief shook his head. "Not really. Our hazmat guys finished their piece just a little bit ago. We've got a crane and a semi trailer on the way to offload the container and take it to a secured warehouse. Then we'll tow the boat itself to a secure docking area."

"A semi and a crane?" Bolan asked. "That's about as inconspicuous as all these lights."

"Our options are limited. Seles wants the Feds to be able to examine the container separately," Cline explained. "And the damn thing weighs a ton."

"He's a by-the-book guy," Bolan replied. "But this doesn't make a bit of sense. Call off the crane and the trailer, have them meet you at the secured docks and offload the container there. The extra time that will take will be worth the extra security. Let's not draw any more attention to the area than we have to."

"I agree with you, sir, but I'm going to need authorization from Agent Seles before I give that order."

"Call him and get it or I will, but just hold off the semi and crane until you do. Worst case, they've got to sit for a few minutes beside the road."

"I can do that," he said. He pulled a phone from his belt and made the call for the incoming crane and semi to hold position. "Just get me the authorization, Agent Cooper. This is too serious for me to screw up."

"I understand," Bolan said, his eyes moving to the body bags. "I'm surprised that they haven't moved the victims. What's taking the coroner so long with the bodies?"

"They're out on the ambulance in ten minutes or less," he said. "We wanted to do a complete search to make sure the bodies weren't carrying something harmful."

"Good call," he said. "But if it's all right, I'd like to take a quick look at them before the coroner removes them."

"Right this way," he said.

Each of the bodies was zipped into an individual black bag and the coroner was beginning to load the first one onto the stretcher.

"Dr. Beaman," the chief said as they stepped closer. "This is Agent Matt Cooper with the DEA. He'd like a moment to examine the bodies, please."

Beaman looked like a man out of patience and way too old for wandering along a cold, rocky beach in the middle of the night. "Young man, if you're about to tell me that there has been yet another delay in getting these bodies back to the morgue I'm going to perform the autopsies right here and let the gulls have the carcasses." The flustered doctor crossed his arms over his chest, huffed at Chief Cline and sent angry glances at Bolan, certain that he was the cause of his having to stay out in the cold.

"No, sir," Cline said. "At least, not for very long. Agent Cooper here just has a couple of questions for you."

"Well, there's not much I can tell you yet. Two of the men appear to have died from gunshot wounds and the other was knifed, but I won't have a lot more until I get them on my table." Beaman looked pointedly at his watch.

"I'd like to take a look," Bolan said.

The coroner sighed as he reached forward and unzipped the body bag and pulled it open to reveal the face of the first victim. Bolan was stunned when he recognized the face and it must have shown.

"You know the guy?" Cline asked.

"I'll have to double-check my files, but I believe he's a lower-level dealer that I've been looking for. Let me see the other two."

The coroner revealed the other two faces. Bolan took quick snapshots and thumbprints from each man with his handheld and sent them off to Brognola to begin the facial recognition and fingerprint ID process. The databases at Stony Man Farm were much larger and more detailed than anything that Seles would have access to.

"When you get them on your slab we're going to need pictures of any tattoos and scars right away and I'll get my people working on it," Bolan said. He handed Beaman a card with his number on it. "Send them digital to that number."

"Won't Special Agent Seles's men already be working on it?" Dr. Beaman asked.

"My people are faster."

"I thought we were all one people working together?" the doctor quipped.

"Sometimes I get to jump the line, that's all," Bolan said. "I won't hold you up any longer, Doctor. You look like you're ready to get out of the cold."

"That's the best news I've heard all night." Dr. Beaman turned to his two assistants. "Load them up and let's get going. We've got a lot yet to do."

Bolan and the chief stepped away as they loaded the bodies. Bolan took a quick look around the ship, but nothing else jumped out at him. It was an expensive piece of work, though, and that meant somebody had paid someone else to do it. He'd be sure to mention it to Brognola as a possible information angle. The money trail was sometimes the easiest one to follow.

"You really did know that kid?" the chief asked. "What a shame. He couldn't have been more than twenty or so."

"I'd never met him, no, but he dropped off the radar about a couple of months ago. I've been working a drug-interdiction case and I never forget a face. That kid was in the briefing files I received." He looked around the beach once more, contemplating all the law enforcement in the area and thinking about secondary strikes. "I'm done here, Chief, and I think you want to move fast to get all this out of sight. I've got a feeling that this just got more complicated. I just wish I knew how."

"I'm on it," Cline said, then spun and headed toward his men, barking orders as he went.

Bolan climbed into his car and dialed Seles.

"Seles."

"Denny, it's Cooper. I have some additional information."

"I'd take some good news right now, so shoot," he said.

"I'm not sure how good it is." Bolan relayed the information about the dead man he knew to have been involved in the local drug trade, as well as his orders to Chief Cline to minimize emergency personnel, cut back on the lighting, and have the container unloaded in a secure area.

Seles sighed heavily. "Jesus, Matt, you're right. I should've thought of all that, thanks."

"It's not a problem. You've got a lot on your plate, Denny. Just get Chief Cline his authorization."

"Done. Do you have any leads on who that kid hung around with? Someone you can talk to for information?"

"He's got an older brother in the 8 Mile area. I'm going to go and snoop around, see what I can get from him. I'm also going to send you what I have now in my files—just in case."

"Is talking to him going to blow your other operation? I can go talk to him myself," Denny said.

"I'll do it," Bolan replied. "I've got a feeling that if we don't get a handle on this situation and fast, there may not be any other cases here…ever."

THE DRIVE FROM THE EOC to the warehouse on the edge of the 8 Mile region gave Michael Jonas ample time to relax and become himself once again. By the time he arrived at the metal building with the boarded-over windows, he was fully Sayid Rais Sayf again, ready to lead his men and fulfill their plans. The building itself was unremarkable from the street and an ownership search would lead the searcher to a shadow corporation within a shadow corporation. In point of fact, it was owned by an unremarkable bureaucrat in the Iranian government who had no idea he was the owner of a warehouse in Detroit, Michigan.

Sayf used the small building behind the eight-foot-high chain-link fence as an occasional meeting place or storage facility, and, at the present, it was his primary office for their mission until it was over, unless something went wrong or they were discovered and forced to move. After he passed through the electronic gate and ensured that it shut behind him, he drove the Audi around to the backside of the building where a garage door opened in response to the button he pressed on his visor.

He parked the car and shut the garage door. From where he was, he could see Malick Yasim through the glass door of the office. He was pacing and, in the reflection from the light, beads of sweat were visible on his bald head. The damage done by the Coast Guard finding the ship was containable, but he couldn't let his second in command see that fact right away. First, he must be reminded of how simple mistakes could cost them everything.

Sayf calmly stepped out of the car, retrieved his briefcase from the backseat, and shut the doors. Yasim would be waiting for his judgment—he was a loyal soldier. But his carelessness had given more information to the authorities than they'd planned, and that could prove crucial to their timing. He crossed the concrete floor of the nearly empty warehouse to the office and opened the door.

Yasim turned to him immediately. "Sayid, I heard about the boat and the bodies. We left it anchored. I did not expect it to come ashore until after everything was completed. I have failed you."

"You are a stupid fool!" Sayf snapped. "Do you know what this means to us? We must change the times for everything and we must keep them looking in other directions. Your mistake makes things more difficult than they already were! What do you have to say for yourself?"

"I…I am sorry, Sayid," the bald man stammered. "Allow me to redeem myself in your eyes. Give me a task to complete to show you that I will not fail you again."

Sayf allowed himself to the luxury of appearing to consider Yasim's words while he put his briefcase on the desk and turned on the computer. "Perhaps there is a way…"

"Anything!"

"What we will need is a diversion, Malick. Something to force the authorities to concentrate on more than one task at a time."

"Yes! This is easily done. I will prove myself to you by creating the diversion you need!"

Sayf sighed and got to his feet, clapping the man on the shoulder. "Easy, my friend. Slow down. I know that you are sorry. Mistakes happen, but we must not allow ourselves to falter foolishly. In any case, we must adjust and I already have a plan in mind that should suffice. You need only to carry it out."

"What must I do?" Yasim asked.

"I want you to take a group of our people to the far end of 8 Mile and start a fight there with one of the other gangs. One of the motorcycle groups if you can. Make it loud, get some fires going, and don't be afraid to kill. Extra bodies will only add to the list of things the authorities must deal with and consider."

The man nodded. "I know a good place for this. When do you want this to happen?"

"Get started now. I want the fight in full swing within an hour. Can you do this?"

"Yes, it shall be done. I will leave immediately and contact you when it's over."

Sayf shook his head. "Go there and get the fight started, but do not linger. I want you back here as soon as possible."

Yasim bowed low and left the office without another word, eager to prove his worth once more. Sayf returned to the desk and sat down, steepling his fingers beneath his chin. In spite of the minor setback, things were moving along well.

Soon, Detroit would explode in a ball of radioactive fire, and become a permanent symbol of the failures of American policy in the Middle East. And as a martyr to the holy cause, he would be revered for all time and rewarded in heaven.

5

Bolan drove from Grosse Point back to 8 Mile, parking half a block down the street from the address in his files. Mr. Tarin Kowt was five feet, ten inches and 180 pounds of pure trouble. He glanced through the man's rap sheet one more time. He'd done a brief stint for theft, but whenever he'd been charged with anything more serious, the witnesses had all somehow magically disappeared. So in spite of three murder charges and five smuggling charges, every single case had been dropped for lack of evidence.

Bolan let his eyes scan the street once more. Even though it was only 8:30 p.m. and a Saturday night, anyone who wasn't part of the problems plaguing this area was already safely tucked inside. The 8 Mile region was a haven for criminals, drugs, prostitutes and numerous types of gangs. The police entered the area only when absolutely necessary, and according to what he'd heard, it was actually better these days than it used to be. It was sort of amazing that this kind of place could exist in an American city, but he'd seen it time and again, in places like Chicago, New York, Boston and even Phoenix.

The rules here were the same as in all those places—keep to yourself and your own crew, don't ask questions, never give answers to the cops, and maybe you and your family will get to live another day. Maybe. No matter what, he suspected that dealing with Kowt would be no simple task.

From where he was parked, the Executioner had a good visual on the house and the street. There was only one vehicle in the driveway—a black Lexus sedan that was probably stolen. Reaching into the gear bag in the passenger seat, he pulled out a RAZ-IR NANO Thermal Camera. This was a handheld model, and he took his time working across the visual field. There were three people inside, and it was likely that at least a couple of them were armed. People like Kowt didn't spend much time without a weapon close at hand. He waited and watched, but the luck of having any of them leave was not on his side and for a reason he would be hard-pressed to name, there was a growing sense of urgency in his gut that told him he needed to move quickly.

Checking his Desert Eagle, Bolan dug around in his gear bag until he found what he wanted, then stepped out and locked the car, activating the alarm system. He was already wearing black clothing, jeans and a wool sweater, with a canvas coat over the top. For the moment, the street was empty. He crossed over, his long strides carrying him from shadow to shadow along the cracked and broken sidewalk. It took him less than three minutes to reach the house, and he opted for a more direct approach.

Pulling the pin, but not releasing the lever from the smoke grenade in his pocket, Bolan walked up to the door and rang the bell. When he didn't hear a tone, he used his left hand to rap sharply on the door. Inside, there was the sound of people scrambling about, and finally, a voice snapping, "Answer the door, you idiot! Cops don't knock!"

The sound of the door being unlocked followed and it opened, revealing the face of a young black man, maybe twenty-five. "What you want, homey?" he asked.

"I have a delivery here for you," Bolan said. "Mr. Jones, right?"

The man's eyes peered about the small porch. "What delivery? Ain't no Mr. Jones here!"

"This one," Bolan replied, pulling the grenade out of his pocket and releasing the lever. "Here." He shoved it into the man's hands, then pushed him backward and yanked the door closed.

The yelling started almost immediately as the man juggled the unwelcome surprise, bobbled it then dropped it on the floor before realizing that it was a grenade and kicking it away.

A voice screamed, "Are you crazy?" even as someone tried to open the door, which Bolan held shut. Through the narrow pane of glass in the door, he could see the room filling with smoke, and hear the chaos as the three men tried to figure out what was going on while simultaneously trying to escape.

The pressure from the person on the other side of the door increased, and Bolan finally let go, allowing it to fly open. It struck the surprised man on the other side with significant force, cracking him in the forehead and splitting the skin. Blood poured freely from the wound and he stumbled back, blinded and stunned. Bolan finished him with a solid right hook to the jaw that dropped him to the floor.

His sudden appearance was enough to get the other two men turned in his direction, but not nearly fast enough. He kicked the door shut behind him, and had his Desert Eagle out in a flash. The two men started to go for their own weapons, but he snapped, "Don't do it. You're dead men if you do."

They both stopped and slowly raised their hands.

"Good," he said. "A wise choice. We'll just wait a minute for the smoke to settle down, then we'll have ourselves a talk." He looked them over. Both men were of Middle Eastern descent, but the one on the right was Tarin Kowt.

"You," he said, gesturing to the man on the left. "What's your name?"

"Aamil," he said.

"So, are you Kowt's workman then?" he asked, knowing the meaning of the name.

"Just a friend."

"Friends are nice," Bolan said. "Come over here. And Kowt, don't even think about going for your piece on the table."

Aamil moved closer, keeping his hands raised. When he was a few feet away, he stopped. "Good," Bolan said. "Now turn around and face your friend."

He complied.

"Do you know much about your friend, Kowt?" he asked.

Aamil shrugged. "Not so much," he answered.

"He's a drug dealer, Aamil," he replied, his voice low and threatening. "More of a mid-level guy these days. His supplier imports directly from Afghanistan, and the question I have for you is, how good a friend are you with him?"

"I..."

"Shut up, Aamil," Kowt said. "I do not know who you are, my friend, but all this violence is unnecessary. Aamil is simply one of my...couriers. I am sure we can come to some arrangement that will satisfy you."

"A bribe, is it?" Bolan asked. "Is that what you're offering me? Money?"

Kowt shrugged. "You act like a cop, and I've bought any number of them in my day. I assumed that's why you came in the way you did. Threatening my friends, waving a big gun around."

Bolan laughed and he saw Aamil stiffen at the sound. "I'm not here for a payoff, Kowt."

"Then what is it you want?" he asked. "A piece of the action? Have I wronged you somehow and you've come seeking revenge?"

"Information exchange," he said. "I tell you something, you tell me something."

Kowt nodded in understanding. "Fine. May I put my arms down now? They are getting tired."

Without a word of warning, Bolan used the butt of the Desert Eagle to rap Aamil once, across the back of the head. He went down without a sound. "There. Now we can talk privately."

"That was unnecessary," Kowt chided, lowering his arms slowly.

"I'm sure Aamil is a prince among men," Bolan said. He gestured with the Desert Eagle. "Sit down."

Kowt moved to the chair, and Bolan quickly checked the room, finding two handguns, a satchel about a quarter filled with cash and plastic tubes that contained brownish-black liquid heroin. "Quite a bundle there," he commented.

"Take what you like, friend," he said. "A gift, if you will. Only, tell me your name, so I may know to whom I have given a gift."

"You can call me Mr. Clean," Bolan replied. "I'm the man they send to clean up messes, and I'm here to work on yours."

Kowt shrugged artfully, his thin shoulders lifting and lowering in a helpless gesture. "I am unaware of any mess that belongs to me," he said, peering around exaggeratedly.

"You are aware of your brother, yes? Sulayk? The one that's been…traveling these past few months."

"I have a brother Sulayk," he admitted.

"Had," Bolan corrected. "He's dead."

Kowt's eyes widened in anger, and Bolan was pleased to see a more emotional reaction in the man. He wondered if Kowt was high or simply secure in his own small kingdom. "Dead?' he whispered. "How can… He is not even back from his trip yet."

"He came in earlier today, mid afternoon or early evening. Where was he?"

"I cannot say. Sulayk doesn't…didn't work for me."

"You're lying to me, Kowt," Bolan said. "So far, this has been relatively pleasant. If you lie, it's going to get unpleasant quickly. One more time. Where was Sulayk?"

"I told you, I cannot say. Not for certain. Somewhere in the Middle East."

Bolan offered a mock *tsk-tsk* sound in reply. Keeping the Desert Eagle aimed at the man, he removed a pair of cuffs from his belt, then started toward Kowt, who began to rise. "I wouldn't," he advised him coldly.

Kowt lowered himself into his seat once more, and Bolan cuffed his hands behind him. Once he was secure, he shut the blinds on the front window, then yanked the pull cord out of the mechanism, using it to tie the man's feet to the chair. Examining his work with a critical eye and judging it satisfactory, he moved to lean against the back of the couch and stare at his captive.

"Here's how this is going to go for you," he finally said. "You can tell me what I want to know about your brother and who he was involved with, and I'll walk out that door and give you twenty minutes to clear out before I call the cops to come and haul you in. With that much smack on hand, plus anything else they find, you'll do a long stretch."

"And if I choose to remain silent?" Kowt asked, a mixture of defiance and fear in his words.

"Then I'm going to force you to talk, and if that means I've got to gag you so no one can hear you scream while I cut off pieces of your body, then that's what I'll do."

The silence that followed this stretched out for several long seconds, and when he deemed that he'd given Kowt time to consider his options, he removed the SEAL combat knife from its hidden sheath behind his back. It wasn't a large blade, but it was very sharp, and in skilled hands such as his, deadly.

"Last chance," he said. "Where did your brother go and who was he working for?"

Kowt's lips thinned as he pressed them together and stared hatred in Bolan's direction.

Using the knife, Bolan cut a heavy strip of fabric off the back of the couch, twisting it tightly, then stepped behind Kowt and pressed it against his lips. The man struggled not to open his mouth, a problem Bolan solved by applying his thumb to the pressure point located beneath the jawline. Kowt opened his mouth and the cloth gag slid into place.

The truth was that Bolan didn't believe in torturing people. It had been done to him, he'd seen it done to others, and it was the least effective way of getting information out of a person he knew. Nonetheless, this entire situation had a feeling of urgency to it and he hoped the threat of physical pain and harm would get the information out of Kowt. He needed it now.

"You've chosen the hard way," he said, holding the knife up before the man's wide eyes. "Now there will be pain."

Lightning-fast, Bolan brought the blade up—and he got the desired reaction as Kowt screamed behind the gag.

Bolan paused, then he slowly lowered the blade.

"So, you have a choice to make. I can remove the gag and you can tell me what I want to know, or..." He waved the blade in the air. "I can get back to work."

Kowt shook his head back and forth rapidly, his face pale.

"You'd like to talk now?" Bolan asked.

The man nodded.

"Good," Bolan said, leaning forward enough to slice through the gag.

Kowt spat, trying to get the foul taste of the gag out of his mouth. He continued this for several moments.

"I'm beginning to lose patience," Bolan snapped. "Start talking or I'll begin…"

"Sulayk told me he was going overseas to acquire nuclear materials for the man he worked for. A man named Sayid."

"Sayid who?" the Executioner asked. "Where can I find him?"

"I don't know," Kowt said. "But there are rumors that he's behind the trouble coming tomorrow."

"What trouble is that?" Bolan asked, suspecting the worst.

"A great many of the 8 Mile gangs have been quietly recruited to stir up trouble tomorrow night. Riots, fights, looting."

"Devil's Night in Detroit," Bolan mused. "Isn't that all pretty normal?"

Kowt shook his head. "Some trouble, yes, but recruiting, no. I think Sayid is behind it. Rumor has it that he—"

The shot sounded from behind Bolan, and he saw it strike Kowt in the throat, killing him instantly. He spun toward the door just as Aamil raced through it, shooting wildly over his shoulder and shouting Islamic curses as he went.

6

Denny Seles believed in trusting his instincts, but when they led him into the 8 Mile region of Detroit without backup, he hated having to follow them. There were few places in the world that could make him nervous, and very few in the United States, but driving down 8 Mile Road after dark on a Saturday night was a little bit like following the Yellow Brick Road straight into Hell. Every corner boasted dealers and pimps lurking in the shadows, while gang members—more than he remembered seeing the last time he'd been down this way—walked the streets with weapons hidden beneath their coats and malice on their minds.

At this moment, his instinct told him that Matt Cooper might be on to something and that he was just as alone out here as he was. So, after he'd received the files and given them the once-over, he'd told Allison Hart that he was going to go check on something and headed in this direction. Cooper wasn't a lightweight and he himself was an experienced field agent. If his instincts were leading him in this direction, there was likely a reason. These thoughts were rolling through his mind when the first shot rang out.

Instinctively, Seles ducked below the steering wheel, then guided the big SUV to the curb, even as several more shots were fired. The address that the DEA agent had given was two more houses down and Seles jumped out of the vehicle as a man came screaming out of the house, turning to fire back through the door. Seles didn't pause even as the man hit the ground, tripped, went down and got back up just as Cooper dove through the front door.

The assailant turned to fire a shot, but by then Seles had closed the gap and was much quicker. He drew his .40 caliber Glock 22, fired once and dropped him cold.

Seles crossed the street to his victim, who lay motionless on the sidewalk. Cooper came running forward, holstering his own weapon when he saw him.

"Tell me he was a bad guy," Seles said. "The paperwork's a bitch otherwise."

"How many good guys shoot at houses they're running from?" he answered.

"True enough. Who was he?"

"Someone more important than I thought. I assumed he was a street runner, and just knocked him out. I was questioning the brother of the kid we found on the boat, a guy named Tarin Kowt, and this guy shot him."

"You get anything from the brother before he died?"

"He was just starting to get genuinely cooperative when this guy took him out. He did say something about the gangs from 8 Mile being used by a guy named Sayid. Something about recruiting for Devil's Night. Does that mean anything to you?"

"Well, Devil's Night is more of an urban legend these days. Halloween used to be a real nightmare for police here. A lot of small riots, arson, vandalism, that sort of thing. When it started getting out of hand, the residents themselves took action. They formed neighborhood watches that worked in tandem with police patrols, set up community activities, that kind of thing. It hasn't been a serious problem in quite a while and it's been under control. Let's face it—most of these are inner-city-gang kids and not international terrorists."

"I know it sounds like a stretch—it sounds like it to me just saying it aloud, Denny—but all of this was really well-planned so far. What if this Sayid character is planning on using the gangs to stir things up or help in whatever their real plan is?"

Seles considered it and then shook his head. "You're right, Cooper, but it's more than a stretch. It snaps past the breaking point. All of these gangs have their own allegiances and agendas. Mostly dealing drugs and stealing. You can't get two groups of them in the same room for a half-hour peace meeting without a fight breaking out, and now you want me to think they're working together?"

Bolan shrugged. "I'm not asking you to accept it, just keep it in mind."

"Fair enough, but have you heard anything during your drug investigation to suggest this sort of thing? I mean, weren't you getting pretty friendly with some of the gang members?"

"Not for that kind of information. I was still too new to be trusted with those kinds of details," Bolan said.

"I believe in trusting your instincts as much as the next man, Cooper, but maybe you're going in the wrong direction here. There's well over a quarter of a million Muslims in Detroit, and they aren't all gangbangers, and they sure as hell aren't all terrorists. We're looking for a needle in a needle stack, and this kind of operation coming out of the 8 Mile neighborhood just doesn't make sense." He peered down the street, looking at all the signs of a populated wasteland. "The people here don't have the resources for the kind of operation it takes to buy a yacht like that, let alone weapons-grade nuclear materials!"

Bolan sighed. "I know it's a long shot, and I appreciate you coming down here, Denny." He held up a cell phone. "This belonged to Kowt. I'm going to have my people run the numbers on it, and I'll make sure it gets sent over to you and logged into evidence."

"I'll get the local guys over here to clean this mess up before I head back to the EOC. Where are you headed next?"

Bolan held up the phone. "Wherever this leads me. I'll be in touch."

Seles looked down the street once more, still aware that in spite of what he'd just said, his instincts told him that somehow it was all connected. The question was whether they'd figure it out in time to stop the terrorists. He turned his attention back to the man he knew as Cooper and nodded. "Try not to get yourself killed out there. The air smells like blood tonight."

"In this part of Detroit, it always does," Cooper replied, then jogged down the street toward his parked car.

THE EXECUTIONER DROVE AWAY from where Seles stood and waited for the Detroit police to show up, only somewhat disappointed that the man didn't seem to be taking seriously the possible connection between the drug-running and the terrorists importing nuclear materials. How did he think they paid for it? He found a dark parking lot several blocks down and pulled over, parking deep in the shadows. Then he pulled out his phone and dialed Brognola's direct line at Stony Man Farm. He answered with his usual directness.

"What do you have, Striker?"

"Not as much as I'd like," he admitted, filling the big Fed in on what he'd learned so far, which wasn't much. "Still," he concluded, "I've got Kowt's cell phone. It's unregistered, but I'm still hoping you can run a trace on the numbers in it."

"Does it have a SIM card data file that you could upload to me?"

"No, it's a throwaway model. Nothing fancy."

"All right, just give me the phone's number, and the last number dialed. I'll see what I can do with that," he said.

Bolan gave him both numbers.

"Are you making any other headway?"

"Well, people are shooting at me."

"At least you're getting someone's attention," Hal said. In the background, Bolan could hear the familiar sound of a keyboard clicking away as Brognola worked his magic on the Stony Man Farm databases.

"Here we go," he finally said. "You're right. This is a pay-as-you-go phone, and the name on the account is…Fred Astaire." There was a pause and then, "The last number dialed is unregistered, too."

"Can you ping the last number called and get me a GPS location?" he asked. "I don't need a name, just a place."

"If the phone is still turned on, I should be able to ping it from a cell tower," he said, clicking away. "Yeah, here it is. I'll text you the address. The computer correlates it with an address from your active file."

Bolan waited for the text to come through and looked at the address. "Yeah, I recognize it. That's the home territory of the Devil's Apostles."

"What's their story?" Brognola asked.

"Motorcycle gang, running in several states. They mostly push meth and they're as territorial as the Mafia. I didn't focus on them too much—trying to track down the heroin chain is difficult enough—but I've heard that when it comes to someone horning in on an area they claim as theirs, vengeful doesn't really cover it."

"How do you think they fit into this?" Brognola asked. "Meth is cooked up in a bathtub, but the heroin you've been tracing is coming from overseas. It's not even the same kind of user, is it?"

"Not generally, but it is interesting. When I was interrogating Kowt, he talked about the area gangs being recruited for something and this is certainly a rival gang. I think I'll pay them a visit and see if any of them are feeling as talkative as Kowt."

"Do you want some backup?" Brognola asked. "I can arrange it without a problem."

Bolan considered it briefly, then dismissed the idea for the moment. "The local FBI guy—Denny Seles—is all right, but he doesn't see the connection yet. I'm not even sure I do. At this point, I'm just following my nose. I'll go in, do a little recon and see what I can find out first. If I need help, I'll call you."

"Keep me in the loop, Striker. The President is breathing down my neck on this one."

"When I know something, you'll know it, too," Bolan promised, ending the call. He put Kowt's phone in an evidence bag and tossed it in the backseat, then started the car. It wasn't far to the address Brognola had given him, and the sooner he got there, the faster he might be able to connect the dots between the terrorists and the gangs running the streets of the 8 Mile region.

THE MASTERPIECE WAS almost complete.

The computer monitor on his desk was directly linked to a secure web-cam network that he'd built himself. From any computer, he could log into his encrypted camera system and see anything from the office where he spent most of his days to over a dozen different warehouses where he and his men processed heroin, and even into the homes of some of his less trustworthy associates. He smiled grimly to himself. If he were to be honest, he could even see into the homes of some of his associates that he did trust.

Presently, the camera he was watching showed three men working with deliberate care. The room they were in was small and shielded from prying eyes by multiple layers. The room itself was inside another room, and both were inside a warehouse that on the outside was labeled Packing Peanuts Unlimited. No one, at least so far, had shown the least bit of interest in stealing packing peanuts. Not that getting through the outer security would have been a simple matter, in any event.

On the monitor, the nuclear weapon he would use to strike the most savage blow ever in the war against America was coming together. He'd been on this path for so long, planted in the muddy cesspit of the infidels, and his patience was stretched thin. But on the screen before him, his reward was taking final shape. He smiled once more. His sacrifice would never be forgotten.

Rabah, his hand-picked expert, must have seen that the camera was on, and he moved away from the work table and picked up the cell phone on the desk, pressing the button that allowed it to function as a walkie-talkie.

"Sayid, my friend, our work is progressing. There is no need for you to watch over us so closely. I am certain you have better things to do."

Sayid Rais Sayf smiled. There were some men in the operation who might waver, but Rabah was among the most dedicated of his group. Together they would begin to rid the world of the evil taint that America had allowed to take form throughout their country and many others. "I do not doubt you, my friend. I was merely marveling at your work. It really is beautiful."

And it was—or at least would be when it was finished. At the moment, it was a half-finished sphere that looked a bit like a metal moon with pieces missing from the upper side. The internal core which contained the uranium was still in the container Yasim had used to ship it—locked behind a lead shield with enough coolant to keep the temperature perfectly maintained.

Rabah nodded at the praise, glancing involuntarily at his own handiwork. It truly was a thing of beauty and even when it was detonated and destroyed, the beauty of that destruction would be a sight to behold, indeed.

"Everything is progressing and we will finish on time, provided we get the bridge-wire detonator on schedule," he said.

"You will," Sayf promised. "All will be well. Continue assembling the device and let me know if there are any problems or issues."

"Of course," Rabah said, then set down the phone. Sayf watched on the monitor a moment longer, then shut it off. There was a great deal more to do if he wanted to achieve a Devil's Night that would be a fiery, cleansing blaze of fury.

7

There were at least half a dozen tricked-out Harleys on the front lawn. From custom-painted choppers to Softtails to Road Kings and more, and another handful of cars parked in front of the house itself. These were low riders, two of them El Caminos, with fancy paint jobs and most likely stolen plates. If it weren't for the well-armed riders and drivers of these vehicles, it might be a street-rod show perfect for a city like Detroit. As it was, the members of two gangs were about to crash into each other. The Devil's Apostles were easy to spot with their distinctive back patches on their leather coats. Bolan didn't know the other gang, but the members appeared to be mostly Latinos. The two groups came together with a resounding crash of human flesh and steel.

Sitting in his car, Bolan watched as the fight began in earnest and he contemplated how best to get inside the house. He was about to step out when his phone rang, and he saw that it was Brognola calling him, so he answered.

"I was just going to call you," Bolan said, skipping the preamble. "All hell's breaking loose at the address you sent me."

"What's going on?"

"Is that GPS signal still there?"

"Yeah, it's still live, but I was able to get you infrared satellite. I thought you might want an uplink before you go in."

"Send it to my handheld," Bolan said. "Thanks."

"I'd get a move on," Brognola said. "Current imaging shows that whoever has that phone is moving around inside the house. He might be getting ready to leave, and we'd have to run the triangulation all over again once he left the range of the closest cell tower."

"Keep on him. I'll make my way to him and you can give me the final ID when I'm close. I'm switching over to my headset now. Stand by."

"Standing by," Brognola said.

Bolan checked that his Desert Eagle was secure in his shoulder rig beneath his jacket, then stepped out of his car. The fight was in full swing, moving back and forth across several yards and the street. He didn't want to engage in the brawl, just skirt it and get into the house.

Jogging to a nearby low hedge and keeping to the shadows, he got to the edge of the fight without any trouble, but getting around it was going to be all but impossible. The hedge bordered the property, and Bolan followed it up to the front side of the house where the phone was located then jumped over, staying low and plotting a path in his mind to the door. Without climbing a tall privacy fence—or breaking it down—he couldn't go around to the back, so the front was his fastest option.

He moved along the front of the house, getting about halfway to the door, before the fight swept closer and an obese Mexican wearing nothing above the waist but a leather vest and an upper body covered in tattoos approached him. "Where you going, *pendaho?*"

"It's a nice night for a stroll," Bolan said, taking a step back just as the man pulled a large knife from behind his back.

"Gonna cut you, *gringo,*" the gang member snarled, swinging the blade across his body and lunging forward at the same time.

Bolan spun, letting the blade and the man's arm go past

him, then caught his wrist, twisted the arm, and brought his left elbow down directly on the joint. The man's arm broke with an ugly snapping sound and he screamed, dropping the knife.

Knowing that it was all fight from here, Bolan thrust a snap kick at the man's temple, and he went down, moaning and cradling his broken limb. Bolan turned then, just as the rest of the fight washed over him in a wave. It was nothing but a whirling mass of bodies, most of them holding knives, chains and, in at least one instance that he saw out of the corner of his eye, a garden hose—no doubt packed with wet sand and sealed with lead on either end.

Cursing in both English and Spanish filled the air, along with grunts of exertion and moans and screams of pain. Any minute, someone was going to start in with a gun, and it would be even uglier. Bolan ducked one wildly thrown punch, came up underneath, and drove a fist into the underside of the biker's chin. Spinning, he kicked low and took out the man's knee, jumping over him and bringing himself almost to the front steps.

Two more bikers, both wearing Devil's Apostles patches, were there, going at it with several Mexicans from the rival gang. He picked the closest one, smashing his hard fist into the man's kidney.

He howled in pain, turning toward him, and Bolan made good use of the movement, stepping close enough to get inside his reach. He engaged a double armlock, then pummeled the man's ribcage with his knees. Once, twice, three times, and he heard them crack on the last one. Stunned at the ferocious attack, the biker stumbled back as Bolan released him, then followed up with a straight snap kick to the chest, which made the thug slam into the group in front of the door. The whole pile went down in a heap of thrashing arms, kicking legs and swear words in two languages.

Bolan stepped around them and reached the steps, but as he started up, he felt a hand grip his right ankle, and before he could adjust, he was on his way down. He put his hands out in front of him to ease the impact and keep his face from slamming into the concrete steps, but the blow on his chest was enough to knock the wind out of him.

Rolling left, he escaped the grasping hand, only to look up and see the biker he'd tossed into the pile-up stagger to his feet and start toward him. In the man's right hand, a large, heavy tow chain dangled, and by the moonlight, Bolan could see that concertina wire had been woven between the links. It was a handmade weapon, but could inflict serious damage. He crab-crawled back up the steps, trying to get to his feet and gain some distance.

"You're some kind of bad ass, huh?" the biker said, as he came forward. His brown mustache and beard were soaked in blood—Bolan must have punctured a lung with one of the broken ribs—and the fact that he was still on his feet was a testament to either his will power, strength, or that he was on drugs of some kind.

"You've got me there," Bolan said, getting himself upright. He noted that the man's eyes were unfocused. His face was covered in acne-like sores, and when he grinned, his teeth were rotted. "How's that meth addiction going for you?"

"Shut the fuck up!" the biker roared, swinging the chain in a wide arc, and forcing Bolan to jump back to get out of its reach. "I'll kill you!"

Reaching the top of the steps, Bolan looked around for a potential weapon. The Desert Eagle would do, but he'd prefer not to use it unless he had to. The idea was to get inside and find the guy with the phone before he brought a lot of attention to himself.

Lumbering up the steps, favoring his left side where his ribs had been battered, the biker swung the chain again and again, using a wide X pattern. Even if Bolan stepped inside to try to end this, it was very likely he'd get hit with the wire-wrapped chain at least once. Out of the corner of his eye, he saw that a broom had been left on the far end of the porch, so he jerked his body in the opposite direction and when the biker moved that way, he cut back and reached out to grab it.

Turning, Bolan saw that his attacker was right behind him, and he barely got the broom up in time. The length of chain spun around the handle, wrapping tightly, and the wire blades dug into the wood. That would have to be good enough, Bolan thought. He stepped forward then, using the broomstick as leverage and rapped the man in the nose with it.

The biker's nose broke with a sharp snap and a rush of blood, and he let go of the handle on the chain, screeching in agony as his hands went to his ruined face.

"I guess playtime is over," Bolan said. He held the broomstick with the heavy tow chain coated in concertina wire. He spun it lightly in one hand and, as the biker's eyes came up to meet his, Bolan whipped the handle in a short arc, rapping the man on the jaw. The blades opened him to the bone, and the chain broke it. He went down screaming. Given his condition, Bolan measured one last move, and kicked him hard in the back of the head. That one put him out.

On the lawn, the fight had moved back into the street, and Bolan was alone on the porch. He activated his headset. "Are you still with me, Hal?"

"Standing by. Are you in the house yet?"

"Moving in now. I had some trouble getting to the door."

Stepping quickly past the windows, Bolan reached the front door, which was slightly ajar. Inside, there was also plenty of noise, and from the sounds of it, more fighting. He moved into the entryway and looked into the main living area. There were about ten men in the room, eight watching as two men fought in the center. One from each of the gangs. *Perfect,* Bolan thought.

"Where is he, Hal?"

"He's in the room right in front of you."

"Where? There are at least ten guys in there!" Bolan snapped.

"Hold on and listen for a moment."

A ring tone sounded and Bolan swiveled his head around and spotted his target.

"Got him," he said. Not bothering to shut off his headset, he moved in to intercept. He barreled his way across the room, plowing into the large biker who was holding the phone that had just stopped ringing in his hand. They crashed to the ground, and the Executioner continued the pressure from the fall, applying all of his weight on the man's chest and keeping his forearm pressed against the man's throat.

"I have some questions for you," Bolan said.

The biker thrashed underneath him, knocking him off balance and sucking in enough air to howl his displeasure. Stronger than he looked, he fought like an angry cat, and when they rolled through the already crowded living room, Bolan realized that he needed to end this quickly or his new biker friend would soon have a half-dozen allies to help him out.

He released his hold and jumped to his feet just as the man pulled a knife free from his belt and sliced the air where Bolan's face had been a moment before. The biker swung wildly at first, but then his aim began to get more precise, slicing through the air and finally skidding through Bolan's coat and shirt, scoring a thin cut along his arm and leaving a trail of blood in its wake.

Ignoring the flash of pain, Bolan closed in and used a wrist lock to force the man to drop the weapon. He followed up with a short, sharp punch to the solar plexus, and repeated it a second time. The air rushed out of his opponent's lungs and he sagged to the floor. A final blow to the back of the neck rendered the man unconscious, and Bolan turned his attention to the rest of the room.

He felt nine sets of eyes on him and all of them belonged to people wearing the insignia of Devil's Apostles. He eased his hand toward the Desert Eagle, having no intention of taking them all on, when the sound of rapidly approaching sirens split the night air.

One of them yelled, "Take off!" and everyone headed for the exits. At his feet, the biker he'd taken out groaned as Bolan bent down to take the ringing phone out of his jacket. It was the exact same make and model as the one he'd taken from Kowt earlier—and probably just as useless.

"Damn it!" Bolan snapped, resisting the urge to chuck it on the ground. Instead, he pocketed both phones and made his way back to the door. The night sky was swirling with the bright blue and red lights of law-enforcement vehicles, but he didn't have time to explain his presence. He slipped off the porch and back over the hedge, making his way to his car unseen in the chaos.

The terrorists were still out there somewhere, and he was officially out of leads.

THE BAY DOORS SLID OPEN and bright LED headlights filled the space. Sayf stood, feigning patience, as Yasim parked his vehicle and approached the office. Everything was moving quickly, and there was little room for error. Even having to send Yasim to do tasks like this posed risks to his plans.

He took a deep breath and steeled himself against his emotions. Impatience was for the unbeliever. Impatience was to force something that Allah had not intended, and he was nothing if not a faithful servant. Everyone would know soon the depth of his resolve.

Yasim made his way to the office and stepped inside.

Sayf smiled at the casual grace that accompanied the man's movements—Malick was as deadly as his nickname—the Mummy—and despite the earlier mistake, he would not err again. It was written on his face. Pride and confidence looked much different from panic.

"All is well, sir," Yasim reported.

"Tell me."

"The gang wars are starting and spreading more rapidly than we could have even hoped for. They will last for hours, perhaps even days, and I have several men prepared to keep them going. The 8 Mile Road is an extremely dangerous place right now and the police will be very busy keeping things under any semblance of control."

"Excellent. You have done well. For now, let them run amok and do the damage. Should intervening become necessary, we will do so. But for the moment, this will work in our favor. In the meantime, your next assignment is waiting for you."

Yasim nodded, his eyes bright with excitement. "My men and I will head for the train yard immediately," he said.

Sayf held up a hand to stop him before he could go. "I need you to make a stop along the way. Our friend, Imam Aalim Al-Qadir, has been asking questions. I do not know the source of these questions, but should it be law enforcement, we must direct them elsewhere. Stop by and ensure that he believes the source of those questions should lead to our warehouse by Blackstone Park."

Yasim raised one thin eyebrow. "You have a trap in place?"

Sayf nodded. "I planned for this contingency. The imam is not to be harmed. He believes in his own way."

"I understand."

"Once you arrive at the train yards, it is imperative that you do not act until I give the order, my friend. No one on your team must get impatient or fearful. Everything must go according to plan. If it does not, our mission will fail."

"I swear to you, no one shall act without my permission, and I will await your command to move ahead."

"Excellent," Sayf said, smiling. "Allah be with you."

"And also with you," Yasim replied, turning and leaving the office.

Sayf watched him go. His plan was coming together, and soon holy fire would burn this city to ashes. He and Yasim would die, but their reward would be waiting for them in the next world.

Nothing could stop them.

8

The high-definition monitors lining the front wall of the EOC were lit up with analysis, deployment patterns and a myriad of pictures from both inside and outside the boat. Denny Seles stared at the screens as if trying to piece together a jigsaw puzzle. Allison Hart stood next to him with the same look of contemplation on her face. "It's all..." He shook his head. "Fucking useless, pardon my language."

"You ever get the feeling that you're missing some vital piece of the puzzle and later on you'll discover that it was right in front of you all along?" Hart asked.

"Kind of like now?" he quipped. "There's something nagging in the back of my head about all this, but I can't put my finger on it. All of this—" he waved a hand at the monitors "—feels like a big road to nothing, but at the same time, my gut is twisting in knots. We're missing something crucial."

"I feel the same way. Someone has a plan, and it's not a sit-and-wait one. I just wish that we'd find something to connect all of it. No one's talking, and we're getting nowhere fast."

Seles's cell phone rang, the caller ID pulled up his office and he flipped it open. "Seles."

"Hey, Denny."

It was one of his newer agents, Adrian Rodriguez. After six years in the police department he'd made it into Quantico and showed a lot of promise as a field agent.

"You need to turn to channel seven," he said.

"Why?"

"You'll see."

Seles asked the question while simultaneously pointing to channel seven on the media list for Hart. She punched in the command and changed one of the monitors to the news channel.

BREAKING REPORT… flashed across the screen. A blonde female reporter was gripping her microphone tightly, and doing her best to look poised, as she tried to report through the throngs of people that were moving around her.

"It's absolute chaos down here," she said. "Gang-fighting on this level hasn't occurred since the seventies, but it appears that the Devil's Night is back in full swing—and a day early. We've identified at least three different gangs, and the fighting has spread to several city blocks. Police have begun to set up barriers to try and prevent the violence from spreading even farther, but we saw at least one barricade that was knocked down and a police car that had been tipped on its side, and there was no sign of the officers. A call to Captain Tolles from the Detroit Police Department has not yet been returned."

"Damn it!" Seles shouted, slamming a hand down on the desk.

"What?" Hart asked.

"We had a report that this might happen, but I didn't take it seriously. I'd better get a team together."

Hart grabbed his arm. "I really need you here on this," she said. "Let Captain Tolles handle it, though he should have contacted me by now anyway. Actually I don't know why he hasn't reported in yet."

"These things move fast, Allison," Seles said. "Maybe he hasn't had time. All I know is that this could all be tied together somehow, and if the police can't get this under control and something else happens on top of it, we could be looking at an even bigger mess." He put his cell phone back on his belt. "I'll take a team down there and be back as soon as I have things under control."

"Famous last words," Hart said, her expression thoughtful. "Just remember that if it is all connected, this could be nothing more than an elaborate distraction."

"It still seems like quite a stretch to me," he said, putting on his overcoat. "I'll be back as fast as I can."

THE HEADLIGHTS FROM his black SUV reflected off the asphalt as Seles drove toward the rendezvous point he'd assigned his other team members. The streets were damp and busy as he cut across downtown, doing his best to avoid traffic, which was heavy despite the late hour. Several times, he was passed by police cruisers with their lights and sirens going full blast—most likely headed to the same place he was.

Putting a team together at the last minute was something he'd always been good at, but using trained FBI agents to disband riots wasn't exactly a normal use of bureau resources. But this wasn't exactly a normal situation. The agents weren't going to be very happy, his boss wasn't going to be happy, and to be honest, he wasn't happy. In the time since he'd gotten the call about the grounded vessel from the Coast Guard, all he'd done was run in circles and here he was doing it again. Still, it was all he really could do.

If he didn't chase the leads or put out the fires he could see, then he'd never get to the issues behind them. His phone buzzed and he pulled it from his belt, hooking it in the phone cradle on his dashboard. The number came up as Matt Cooper. So far, Cooper had been the only one actually able to track down anything like a real lead, even if the path had gotten him nowhere so far.

He hit the talk button. "If you're calling to tell me that you were right, Cooper, I'm probably going to shoot you on sight."

"I'm not really the I-told-you-so type, but thanks for the warning," he said. "Either way, all of this is screaming that someone designed it, planned it all well in advance."

"So who's the designer?" Seles said.

"I'm not sure yet," Bolan said, "but I just narrowly escaped one set of the fights they've set off while I was tracking down that cell phone."

"It was a dead end?"

"Handed off to a patsy. The guy didn't even look like he knew he had the phone in his pocket, and it's the exact same type as Kowt was using. Someone's turned hell loose out there and put me down right in the middle of it. I can't wait to return the favor when I find the man responsible."

"Where are you now?"

"Driving to the EOC. I'll give the phones to your techs. Maybe they can get something more off them."

"What's your next move?" Seles asked, stopping as a light turned red.

"I've got a contact to check in with and see what he was able to dig up. I'm hopeful he's got something, otherwise I'm batting zero and out of ideas."

Seles had just started to reply as the light turned green when a massive explosion lit up the sky on his left. Orange, blue and red flames shot into the sky as his SUV rocked from the shockwave. "Oh, God!" he shouted.

"Did you see that?" Bolan yelled. "What the hell was that?"

"An explosion in the train yards. Yeah, I saw the blast. Did you?"

"Everyone in the city might have," Bolan said.

"Skip the EOC," Seles ordered. "I'm going to head to the train yards, and I'd like you there. We may need every hand we can get."

"What about the riots?" he asked.

Seles slammed his foot down on the accelerator and spun a sharp left, turning on his emergency lights and sirens. "I guess we'll just have to do the best we can. We're already spread too thin as it is."

"Got it," Bolan said. "I'll meet you over there as fast as possible."

The line no sooner went dead than it rang again, this time coming up as Allison Hart. Seles hit the talk button once more. "I know," he said without preamble. "I'm already headed that way. Can you scramble fire and ambulance to the scene?"

"It's the Livernois Train Yard," she said. "I'm ordering all available emergency units to the scene now."

Seles yanked the wheel, narrowly avoiding a collision with a slow-moving pickup truck and his tires screeched on the pavement. "What about the riots?" he asked.

"We don't have a choice," she said. "The people there are just going to have to handle things on their own for a while."

"At least it wasn't a nuclear blast," he said. "That's something."

"Do you think this was it?" she asked. "Some kind of train bombing?"

Seles considered it as he blew through a red light, ignoring the sounds of honking from angry motorists who either didn't see or didn't care about his emergency lights and siren. "I don't know," he finally said. "It doesn't make sense. Maybe something went wrong and they blew up the device before it was ready or the uranium didn't work right. That's possible, I suppose."

"Let's hope so," she said. "Just get over there and find out what's going on."

"I'll be there in three minutes," he said. "Just get me everything you can. I don't know how many casualties there'll be."

"Oh, I doubt very many," Hart said, with a relieved sound in her voice. "The Livernois Train Yard is just a switching station for the trains. No passengers go through there."

Seles sighed heavily. "Then this isn't the terrorists," he said. "They like human targets."

"Damn," she said. "You're right. This is just another straw on our backs."

Realizing that Cooper was right, he said, "That's exactly what it is. Another thing for us to deal with—that we *have* to deal with—to keep us from doing the work of tracking the terrorists down. Agent Cooper was spot-on. *All* of this was planned in advance."

The silence on the other end stretched out long enough for him to wonder if they'd lost the connection when she said, "If you're right, then what do we do?"

"I don't know," he admitted. "I guess we take it one emergency at a time and hope like hell that Cooper can bring in a lead that stops them in time."

"That's not much to hang our hopes on," she said.

"For now, it's all we've got." He pulled to a stop three blocks from the train yards. The air was filled with smoke and whatever had exploded was still burning. There was an acrid scent in the air that told him chemicals were involved. "I'm at the train yards now, Allison. Get a hazmat team down here pronto. Whatever they blew up, it had a chemical composition."

"I'm on it," she said, then hung up. Seles continued closer to the source of the explosion, wondering what he was getting himself into by not waiting, then realizing that it didn't matter—he had to make sure no one else was in there.

When the explosion rocked the night sky, Yasim put the van in Drive and slowly moved away from the scene. Eighteen thousand gallons of chromic acid, combined with enough C-4 to derail several train cars, would keep the emergency crews busy for hours. It was highly corrosive, and inhaling the dust could cause everything from severe coughing to death, depending on the concentration.

He drove in large circles, waiting until he saw the first of the emergency vehicles arriving, then pulled away from the scene completely. There was no reason to stay, though he'd find a great deal of pleasure in watching them scurry about like ants confronted with an army of grasshoppers. For the time being, his pleasure would have to be taken in the knowledge of a job well done.

He pulled his cell phone from his pocket and called Sayf. "It is done," he said, when his call was answered.

"Yes," he said. "There is a news helicopter showing it on the television right now. Well done, Malick. They will have no choice but to try to contain the spill…and the riots will continue to grow."

"And we will be undisturbed as we prepare the weapon and deliver it," Yasim finished. "Allah is great."

"Indeed," Sayf said. "And the imam who was asking questions?"

"He will be no trouble. I told him enough to ensure that whoever he talks to will go where we want them."

"Excellent," Sayf said. "Go ahead and go to the warehouse where they are building the device. I'll meet you there in a little while. I have some errands to run first."

"As you command," Yasim said. He ended the call and pulled to a stop as another three fire trucks and an ambulance raced by. In his rearview mirror, he could see the fire and smoke lighting the sky.

It was nothing compared to the holy burning that was coming, but for the moment, it would do. He pulled away from the curb, looking back once more. It would do very well, indeed.

9

The group of men seated at the conference table in the White House situation room listened carefully as Vincent Walker, a Senior Deputy to the National Security Advisor gave his report on the situation in Detroit. So far, he had their complete attention. In spite of, or perhaps because of his time as an actual special operations field agent for the NSA, Walker was a completely political animal. It mattered little to him if the person running the White House was far left, far right or somewhere in between, so long as that person left national security to the professionals.

Walker knew that if he handled this properly, he'd be the next National Security Advisor to the President of the United States. For him, this was just one step closer to his true ambition. At a shade over six feet, he could and did meet the gaze of every man in the room, showing a certain deference to the President himself when he spoke. In the fluorescent lighting, his undyed hair, combed almost straight back, was a mix of willow-bark brown with streaks of white. His suit was tailor-cut and highlighted the fact that he was still in excellent physical condition. Walker ran five miles a day, worked out in the gym with weights at least four days each week and could kill most of the men in the room without breaking a sweat. Very few people intimidated him, and the current President was not on that list.

Still, he showed the deference necessary with his eyes and his body movements. Concluding his report, he said, "Gentlemen, the situation is, in my estimation, bleak. We've got missing weapons-grade uranium, now a train explosion that might or might not be an accident, riots in the 8 Mile region, and—you'll excuse me, please, as I'm sure she's a perfectly competent person—a *woman* with no practical field experience running the show."

"What about Denny Seles?" the President asked. "He's running field operations, right?"

"Respectfully, Mr. President, Special Agent Seles has been running an office for several years. He's out of practice. Frankly, there's no room for mistakes here. We could lose hundreds of thousands of lives if we don't act now."

The President reviewed the files in front of him once more. "I'm inclined to agree with you, Deputy Walker. Allison Hart does lack the experience for this kind of thing, but Seles is well-trained and seems to be doing about as much as anyone could expect under the circumstances. Maybe we should give them a little more time to get a handle on this thing before we send someone in to take over."

"Sir, my fear is that time is the one commodity we can't afford to lose at this point. Whoever is behind this has succeeded in bringing nuclear materials into the United States, and we don't even know yet the extent of the damage they could do. We've got experts running different scenarios, but without a clear indication of the kind of weapon they plan on using, they're just guessing. Detroit is devolving into chaos and this *girl*—excuse me, woman—who is directing the EOC clearly doesn't have the experience to make the decisions that need to be made to put an end to all of this."

"What did you have in mind?" he asked.

"I propose that I go, sir. I know that it's stepping up the federal role, but I don't know that we have a choice at this point. We need to bypass some of the state controls and get a hold of this situation before it gets worse."

"The FBI field office is already involved, and they're reporting directly to Langley. Wouldn't it be easier to have them take over the EOC as well as field operations?" the President asked.

Walker shifted and turned his gaze, allowing it to meet the President's directly. He cleared his throat with a sound that was softly derisive.

"Sir, all they've shown so far is that they do not have the situation in hand. With all due respect to my colleagues, if the FBI had been on their game then these materials would not be on U.S. soil in the first place. It's unacceptable that a terrorist could use a port in the middle of the country to bring in this kind of potential weapon."

"I think there's plenty of inter-agency blame to go around," the President said stiffly. "This wasn't on anyone's radar, including the NSA's."

Walker nodded thoughtfully. "I agree with you, sir. It's an intelligence failure on many levels, but...if these terrorists succeed in detonating whatever kind of weapon they're building, they'll have shown a precedent that our ports—all of them—are vulnerable. We'll have a boat from every terrorist organization in the world in our harbors before the week is out."

"All right, Deputy Walker, you've made your case," the President said. He removed a pen from his suit pocket and signed the order in front of him, authorizing Walker to take over the Detroit EOC temporarily. "You've asked for it and it's yours, but I expect this damn thing resolved quickly."

"Of course, Mr. President," Walker said, keeping a grim smile on his face.

"And do yourself a favor," he added, pointing the pen in Walker's direction. "Keep that Allison Hart woman around and leave Seles in charge of field operations. She may know more than you want to give her credit for, and by all accounts Seles is a damn fine agent himself."

Walker nodded his head in agreement. "I see no need to shake things up too much, sir," he said. "I'm just going to provide some extra oversight and experience that will hopefully allow us to end this situation more quickly."

"Get it done," the President said, then stood and left the room.

Walker took a deep breath. He got to his feet and pulled his cell phone out, hitting the button that would automatically dial his office. His secretary answered on the first ring. He'd kept her on staff for three years because she knew her place. "Charlene, the President just signed the order. Call my driver and tell him to start the car, then call the pilot and tell him to meet me at the airfield in ten minutes. I want us wheels-up in thirty."

"Yes, sir," she said, hanging up without any additional comments.

Walker headed for the exit, nodding absently at the Marine standing guard. It was going to be a long, but very good, night. He felt it in his bones. The situation in Detroit was the perfect opportunity to take a huge leap up the ladder, and maybe get all the way to the top.

FLAMES WERE SHOOTING into the air. Above them, clouds of black smoke roiled while eerie shadows danced over the fire trucks and emergency workers trying to control the scene. Everyone was wearing some kind of hazmat gear, though at the moment, the biggest concern appeared to be controlling the blaze.

Bolan pulled his car over and jumped out, flashing his credentials to the officers blocking the looky-loos and trying to convince them to get out of the area. He skirted the fire trucks and made his way to the small command post that Seles was trying to establish outside the immediate danger zone.

Seles's SUV was equipped with the latest in emergency-response equipment and the smart board sent a faint glow into the throng of responders that were crowding around to hear their orders. The FBI agent appeared calm, but the strain of the day's events was clear in the lines of weariness around his eyes and the tension in his jaw.

"So, everything in terms of transport—that includes injured emergency personnel—is going to run through the EOC. We know this is a chemical spill, as well as a fire, so captains get your people geared accordingly, and if they aren't, I want them pulled out right now," Seles was saying. Bolan waited as the agent carefully walked the captains through the response orders: possible victims were the first priority, then the fire, then the spill.

Bolan noted that the fire chief was looking more than a little disgruntled, and he figured it was because Seles wasn't handing over incident command to him. The man's arms were folded tightly across his chest, and he started to turn away even before Seles had finished talking. Bolan was already tired of the games being played by the terrorists and did not have the time nor the patience to have Seles distracted with the song and dance of a jurisdictional pissing contest.

He sidled up next to the chief and tapped him on the shoulder. The chief looked at him, then turned away, scorn written all over his face. Bolan tapped him again, this time a little harder. The chief wasn't a small man, but Bolan had a good six inches in height on him.

"You got a problem or something to say?" the chief growled.

Leaning in close enough so that only the chief would hear, Bolan whispered, "I have a problem. You are the problem. Right now, this city is falling apart. We've got riots, terrorists, and now this. My job—and Agent Seles's job, for that matter—is to put out *all* the fires. Every single one of them."

"What's your point?" the chief half snarled.

"My point, Chief," Bolan continued, "is that if you don't fall in line in the next ten seconds, fix your attitude and do exactly what you're ordered, I'll take time away from my busy schedule hunting down terrorists and turn my full attention to you. There won't be a rock big enough for you to hide under that will protect you from the storm I will rain down on you." He smiled grimly. "You understand me, Chief?"

Without waiting for an answer, Bolan stepped away from the wide-eyed man just as Seles wrapped up his briefing, and the leaders left to brief their individual teams. The chief walked away with a quick glance at Seles, and a furtive look in Bolan's direction.

"I figured he'd be pissed as a cat in the rain," Seles said. "Instead, he looks like he wants to run for his life. What did you say to him, Cooper?"

Bolan shrugged. "I don't know. We were just discussing the weather."

"The weather?"

"Yeah, you know…rain, storms, that kind of thing." He pointed in the direction of the fires. "Denny, you know this is all a giant distraction, right? Coincidence happens, but not like this."

"I have that same notion," Seles said. "But we're still stuck dealing with the fallout. So far, we haven't found any victims, thank God. But those chemicals are toxic as hell and they'll eat right through damn near anything. The fumes are toxic, too. If the wind was blowing in this direction, we'd be wearing hazmat suits ourselves."

"How long until you can get this situation under control?" Bolan asked. "We've got more important fish to fry."

"I know we do," Seles admitted, "but we're spread out

so thin that I don't know how long it's going to take to get people back in place. I'm hoping we get lucky—or you do. These guys are bold, I'll give them that, but boldness and arrogance are kissing cousins. Maybe they'll make a mistake."

Bolan shook his head. "I don't think we can count on that," he said. "So far, they're playing it perfectly. They've got law enforcement busy with other things, the emergency crews working all over the city, and our focus is everywhere and on everything but them."

"They're playing us," Seles said.

"It's as orchestrated as a symphony concert," Bolan said. "How thin is law enforcement in this city right now?"

Seles sighed. "*Thin* doesn't describe it. *Nonexistent* is closer to the mark in a lot of places."

"So get wrapped up here and let's get our focus back where it belongs—on whoever smuggled the uranium into the country."

The FBI agent nodded. "All right," he said. "I'll get this in hand, make sure we've done a solid evidence sweep, then transfer command to the fire chief. I just don't want us to overlook anything."

"I think you're wasting your time," Bolan said, "but I can see why you want to play it by the book."

"We've still got to *try* and find some evidence. What else do we have at this point?"

"Not very damn much," Bolan admitted, just as his cell phone vibrated. A rush of hope filled him as he saw the imam's number on the screen.

"Cooper, here," he said, raising his voice over the sound of the chaos around him. "Do you have something for me Imam Al-Qadir? Please tell me you do."

"Yes, I have information," he said. "Can you come to the mosque? I will tell you everything I have learned."

Bolan looked at his watch. "I'll be there within twenty

minutes," he said. "Don't go anywhere." He ended the call, then turned back to Seles. "I've got to go."

"If we don't have anything, where the hell are you going?" he asked.

"I just got a lead," he said. "I want to try and end this thing before it gets worse."

"A lead? What kind of a lead?"

"A spiritual one," Bolan said. "I'll call you as soon as I know more." He turned and jogged back toward his car before the agent could ask any more questions. The fire, devastating as it might be, was nothing more than a flare shot into the night. It lit up the sky, but its heat and light wasn't the real danger at all.

10

In spite of the early discovery of the transport vessel carrying the uranium, everything was moving according to his carefully laid plans. Sitting in the parking lot of the EOC, Sayf—once again in his Michael Jonas persona—was dialing Hart's cell phone, knowing that it would likely go straight to her voice mail. Vehicles from every imaginable emergency department were coming and going like angry bees in the parking lot. The lobby would be chaos.

Yasim's success at getting the riots going was being rapidly overshadowed by the massive response being created by his train explosion. In spite of driving well in excess of the speed limit—and passing by three marked police cars—Sayf hadn't been stopped once. They didn't even slow down to look at him, their minds in more important places.

As he expected, Hart's voice mail answered his call. He hung up, rather than leave a message she was unlikely to hear for some time to come. Besides, he had every intention of going inside and seeing for himself how the situation was developing within the emergency operations center. He checked his watch and saw that it was just a few minutes after one in the morning. If everything went according to schedule, in a little over fourteen hours, the bomb he intended to detonate would explode, taking thousands, perhaps hundreds of thousands of lives.

In order for that to happen, Sayf had to ensure that every branch of law enforcement and emergency management was busy with other urgent problems. While they wouldn't lose sight of the uranium, a potential emergency was a far different thing than one actually happening. And there were going to be more emergencies to keep everyone occupied so that he could finish building and putting the bomb in place.

Sayf adjusted his tie in the mirror, then stepped out of the car, locking it behind him with the button on the key fob. The car was an extravagance he afforded himself—part of the image of Michael Jonas—but he did enjoy driving it. Sayf would never allow himself such luxuries, but Michael Jonas could and did enjoy the finer things in life. Sayf would miss them, but the rewards waiting for him in heaven would be tenfold, a hundredfold, more luxurious than any he had enjoyed on earth.

Crossing the parking lot, he ignored the occasional person who passed him and confidently entered the EOC lobby. This time, he was prepared with a more direct approach, and fortune was smiling on him. Despite the hours, Officer Robards was still on duty, and offered him a tired grin when he got to the desk.

"Mr. Jonas," he said. "What brings you back in this late?"

He shared his own weary smile with the man. "My guess is that my reasons are the same as yours for still being on duty. The owners at the field are up in arms about the train explosion—it's not far from the stadium, as you know—and so here I am." He gave a shrug. "If Allison can spare even a minute…"

"Let me ring her line," Robards said. "I'll tell her you're here."

Sayf turned away and moved several feet back, to give the officer the space to make the call. Every physical gesture was important in a situation like this. Robards was tired and by moving away, Sayf ensured that he was showing respect to the situation. He could hear the man speaking into the phone on his desk, then hanging up.

"Mr. Jonas?" he called.

Sayf turned around. "Yes," he said, moving closer.

The guard removed a credit-card-size visitor badge with a magnetic strip on the back from a drawer. Typing a quick entry on the computer in front of him, he swiped the card through a reader on top of the desk. "She told me to send you to her office. You've been back there before, right?"

"Many times," he said, taking the offered badge. "I just swipe this on the reader, right?"

"Yes," Robards replied. "It's logged to your name. Swipe it before you go in, then again when you come out and return it to me."

"Thanks very much," he said, swiping the card as instructed. "I won't be long."

"It's crazy back there," the guard warned. "Every man for himself."

"Then I'll do what I can to keep my own crazy to a bare minimum. I wouldn't want to add to Allison's burdens."

"You're a wise man, Mr. Jonas," he said. "Especially if you want to keep dating her."

"Oh, indeed," he replied, moving toward the hallway that led into the heart of the EOC. Even in the lobby, he could hear the sound of computers and people working at a highly intensified pace. Still, it didn't prepare him for the sight that greeted him when he moved into the main auditorium area. Every station was operational, and several previously empty stations had been set up for temporary use. He guessed there might be as many as a hundred people in the main room, working the phones and computers. On the wall-mounted monitor displays, he saw several projections related to the fire, two dedicated to the riots, and—at the moment—only two running scenarios related to his true aim.

Hart was in her glass-walled office at the top of room, and when he caught her eye and waved, she motioned for him to come that way. He nodded pleasantly at several people he knew by sight, if not name, and stepped into her office. She was listening intently to the phone she held to her ear and motioned for him to sit down.

Sayf took a seat, watching curiously as the agent's face went through several expressions ranging from dismay to anger, and ultimately settling on a weary sort of acceptance. Her office was usually as neat as a driven perfectionist could make it, but on this night, file folders were stacked haphazardly on the top of her desk, a file-cabinet drawer was open, and her white blouse was open at the neck and wrinkled from hours of wear. Her hair was in need of a good brushing. In short, she and her space looked a mess.

"I understand, sir," Hart said into the phone. "I'll do everything I can to make the transition easier. I just want it on record that I formally object to this action and I'll be stating that in my final report."

Sayf smiled at her encouragingly, but he was concerned about the word she'd used—*transition*.

"Yes, sir. Good night, sir." Hart hung up the phone and sighed heavily.

"Are you all right, my dear?" he asked.

"As good as anyone in this mess could be who's just been demoted," she said, as she stared off into space.

"I... Demoted, you said?"

"Yes. That was the Director of the National Security Agency, Dean Edward Talbot, Senior. The President has ordered that one of the deputy directors, a man named Vincent Walker, is to take over operational command here as soon as he arrives."

"I'm so sorry, Allison," he said. "It seems to me—given everything that is going on—that you are doing the best you can. No one can ask for more than that."

She started to reply, stopped herself, then slammed her hands on top of the desk. Taking a deep, calming breath, she shook her head. "My best isn't good enough, and the truth of it is that they're right," she said. "I'm out of my depth here. If Denny Seles wasn't needed in the field, maybe he could take over, but right now, I've got to have someone out there I can trust."

"How bad is it?" he asked. "In the field, I mean?"

She sighed again, then leaned back in her chair and ran her hands through her already mussed hair. "Bad. We've got riots popping up over on 8 Mile Road, but once the police arrive, everyone just disappears. We've got a train accident that may be a bombing, and the cars were filled with a toxic chemical that causes burns, just for a start. Oh yeah…and weapons-grade uranium has been smuggled into the city by terrorists."

She started gathering files together and stacking them neatly on the desk, more, he thought, to give her hands something to do than anything else. "It sounds like a…like a bad movie," he suggested. "That's a lot for one night."

"It's insane!" she snapped. "There has to be a connection, but damned if we know what it is or where to look. We're stretched to the breaking point. God forbid anything else goes wrong."

Sayf pondered her words and the implications of her being demoted. He would have to adjust his plans a bit, he decided. Having Hart in charge was to his benefit because—as she knew herself—she wasn't qualified for this level of an emergency. One of the three she could handle, but things were spiraling out of control. "Well, I do not want to bother you. The stadium owners called me when they heard about the fire.

It's not all that far from the stadium and they expressed concern. They *asked*—I use the word facetiously, of course—me to come down and find out if we need to cancel the game."

"You're not a bother, Michael," she said, getting to her feet and straightening the last of the files in a neat stack. "You've got a job to do, too, and when that many people are gathered at a public event, we want them to be safe."

"I appreciate your understanding," he said.

"Let me show you what it looks like, so you can reassure everyone," she said. She turned the monitor around so he could see it and tapped a series of keys, bringing up an overlay of the city. "Here's where the fire is in relation to the stadium," she added. The stadium was suddenly highlighted in blue, and the area of the train yards in yellow.

"The wind is blowing in the opposite direction, and Denny reported in about ten minutes ago that they think they'll have it under control by morning. Fortunately, the only injuries so far have been to firefighters and law enforcement, not to civilians." She added the wind overlay, then a time-release component, showing the spread of the fire, and the image slowly shrank back down. "Everything should be fine for… I guess it's later today, isn't it?" she asked.

"Indeed," he said. "I appreciate the reassurance. Would it help you to have me call in my security staff from the stadium? They are well-trained, and could help with security around the fire, at least."

She tapped a fingernail thoughtfully on her teeth, then shook her head. "Unless something else breaks, I think we're going to get through this. I'd rather you have your people focused on the stadium. When people start showing up for tailgating and getting ready for the game, they're going to want a lot of reassurance. How are you staffed?"

"I already ordered everyone in for the game, so we'll have

almost twice the usual security presence prior to kickoff," he said. "I'll ensure that everything is kept calm and safe."

"Good," she said. "Maybe by then, we'll have this mess under control."

He got to his feet, satisfied that everything was moving in the direction he desired. "I'm certain you will," he said. "Is there…anything else I can do?"

"Just kiss me good-night, then go get some sleep. God knows I wish I could do the same."

He kissed her lightly on the cheek. "As do I," he said. "Good night, Allison."

She allowed herself to be held briefly, then her phone rang and she pulled away. "Good night, Michael. Just text if you need anything else. I've got so many phones ringing…" She answered the one on her desk, telling the person to hold. "I've got my phone on vibrate, so send a text. I'll read it and get back to you if it's urgent."

"I imagine I'll do my best to stay out of your way the rest of the night. I have my hands full as it is, with anxious stadium owners."

"Thanks," she said. "Good night, Michael. I've got to take this."

"Yes, of course," he said. He turned and left her office, walking back out through the auditorium, and stopping long enough to reswipe his card and hand it back to the desk officer. He bade the man a good night, then returned to his car.

Everything was going as expected, except Hart's demotion. He would have to do something about that, and very soon. It wouldn't do to have anyone competent running the EOC. That simply wouldn't do at all.

He drove back in the direction of the warehouse, contemplating the steps necessary in ensuring that Hart's replacement wouldn't get in the way, and then, when he'd reached a decision, removed one of the disposable cell phones from the console, dialing a number from memory.

When the other person answered, Sayf said only a few words. "Prepare a vest, Malick, and find a volunteer with the courage to do what he must."

11

Imam Al-Qadir was waiting for him by the back door of the mosque when Bolan arrived, and he gestured for him to hurry inside. Curious at the man's urgency, he moved quickly inside and followed a mostly silent Al-Qadir back to his office, where the man shut the door and pulled down the blind. For a moment, it looked as if he was considering locking the door, too, but then he shook his head and stepped over to his desk, where he sat down. This was a different man than Bolan had met earlier in the day. That man had been open and friendly. This one was scared of something.

"Thank you for calling me," Bolan said. "I know you care about the people of this community."

"I…admit that I hesitated before calling you," the imam said. "When I tell you what I have learned, perhaps you will be angry at me that I waited nearly an hour before I dialed your number."

"I doubt it," Bolan said. "You're obviously scared, and scared people—in my experience—don't always make fast decisions. I'm just glad you made the right one when you did."

"I knew that to call you was right," he said, "and you are right, too. I am scared. I have been watching the news today and it's been impossible to miss what's happening on the streets outside. If these men have their way, it will only get worse. Perhaps much worse."

"So you have a name for me?" Bolan asked.

"Better," the imam replied. "I have an address. The person I spoke to told me that this is where the bomb is located." The imam started to hand Bolan a half sheet of paper, then stopped. "Agent Cooper, you have always seemed to me to be an honest man, a good man. But I wish to ask you something before I give you this information."

Bolan nodded. "Of course."

"Will you give me your word that you will do your best to arrest the men behind this, and see to it that they get a fair trial?" The imam's question was a good one. Given his place in the community, it was even a fair one.

"Anyone that I catch," Bolan said, choosing his words carefully, "will be given every opportunity to exercise their rights."

The imam was not stupid, and Bolan didn't think he'd accept that. "I did not ask you if whoever you find would be given the chance to exercise their rights. I asked if you would do your best to arrest them and see to it that they get a fair trial."

For a moment, Bolan thought about sugarcoating his response, but ultimately chose not to. The imam deserved as much of the truth as he could give him. "Imam Al-Qadir, my friend…I will try to arrest them, but it seems very unlikely that they will surrender. If they do not, I won't risk the safety of this country or this city, or even myself, begging them to play fair. Men like this don't play fair. If they resist, I'll be the only trial they get."

The imam thought about Bolan's words, then nodded, holding out the paper. "I understand," he said. "I only ask that you try."

"On that, you have my word," Bolan said.

"Good," Al-Qadir replied, passing him the sheet of paper. On it was the address for a warehouse closer to the western end of 8 Mile Road, in an area he knew was filled with boarded-up warehouses. "How reliable is this information?" he asked.

The imam shrugged. "I can only tell you what I was told. That inside the building at that address, there is a group of people building a bomb of some kind."

"Can you tell me who told you this?" he asked. "A name would help a lot."

The imam shook his head. "I cannot. I gave my word that he would remain anonymous. If I am to succeed in this community, people must know that they can trust me when I tell them I will protect their confidentiality."

Bolan nodded his head. It made sense, but that didn't mean he had to like it. "I guess it will have to do. I can check it out and see what's there. Right now, it's the only lead we've got."

"You will go alone?"

Bolan considered that, then said, "Probably not. I'll bring in a reliable man to help me."

"Please remember your promise," the imam said, getting to his feet. "And I can sense that you wish to leave, so please, go and go safely. May Allah watch over you."

Bolan stood and shook the imam's hand. "If you hear anything else, anything at all, please call me right away. If this doesn't pan out, we're going to be up the creek without a paddle. Hell, we won't even have a canoe."

"I understand," Al-Qadir replied.

They walked to the back door together, where the imam let him out. Bolan waited until he reached his car and was safely inside, before he dialed Seles's number. The FBI man answered on the second ring, sounding even more wrung out than earlier.

"Agent Seles here," he said.

"Denny, it's Matt Cooper. I've got a lead—and it's a hot one."

"Tell me," he said.

Bolan filled him in on his meeting with the imam. "If you can put a team together, we can meet there and go as soon as you're ready."

"Twenty minutes," Seles said. "We'll come in quiet. Look for my SUV and a large cargo van with Sunshine Cleaning painted on the side."

"I'll be there," Bolan said. "Maybe we can end this night on a high note."

"At this point, I'd just settle for it coming to a good end," Seles replied, then hung up.

Bolan started the engine and headed for the address on the sheet of paper. With any luck at all, the terrorists would be taken down in less than an hour. He hoped he'd be able to keep his promise to the imam, but in his experience, surrender wouldn't be an option for the terrorists any more than it would be for him.

The biggest difference was that these were terrorists and he was the Executioner. He pressed the accelerator. It was time to do what he did best.

BY ALL APPEARANCES, the warehouse hadn't been in use in months, maybe years. The sign that had once been painted on the wall facing the road was faded and illegible. A six-foot-high chain-link fence surrounded the building, and there was both a vehicle and pedestrian entrance. From where Bolan was parked, both looked as if they were locked with a heavy length of chain and a padlock. The building itself wasn't lit on the outside and the narrow row of ventilation windows along the top were also dark. An old delivery van that had been white at one point in its existence was presently a mottled gray-and-rust-splotched wreck standing on at least two flats. He didn't see any other vehicles on the other side of the fence, and by all appearances, the place was long deserted.

If the terrorists were hiding in there, they were keeping a profile so low that it was invisible from the street. Of course, Bolan thought, that's pretty much the point. He scanned the building one last time with the night-vision goggles, then shook his head. The only way to know for sure would be to go in and have a look.

He checked the Desert Eagle and replaced it in his shoulder rig, then slipped a freshly sharpened blade into the top of his boot. Down the street, he saw Seles's large SUV coming, and he flashed his headlamps once. In response, the FBI agent shut off his own and slowed, pulling to a stop facing Bolan's vehicle. The Executioner got out and met Seles between the vehicles.

"Cooper," Seles said, nodding. "Have you seen anything?"

Bolan shook his head. "Nothing, but it's a pretty well-sealed building. I don't have infrared, just night-vision, but from what I can tell, it looks deserted. Maybe the information I got was bad."

"We'll know more in a minute. I've got three guys on the other side of the building. Hang on." He tapped his earpiece and said, "Blue Team, do you copy?"

Bolan couldn't hear the other side of the conversation, but assumed someone answered because Seles continued talking quietly. "Go to infrared sweep on the building. If you get a hit, let me know. Until then, everyone holds position."

They waited for a couple of long minutes, then Seles said, "Go ahead." A moment later, he grinned. "Confirmed. Stand by."

"Good news?" Bolan asked.

"There are four people inside on the main floor, two on the upper floor—looks like they're walking guard rounds. That building has been made to appear rundown and abandoned on purpose."

"Only six?" Bolan asked, thinking that for the kind of operation he thought they were dealing with, six seemed like a small number.

"That's what came up on the infrared," Seles said. "It's possible there's some kind of underground level, but my spotter wouldn't be able to see it."

Bolan considered this, then nodded. "We've got to go in anyway, so let's take them alive if we can. I think we've both got some questions we'd like answered."

"Agreed," he said. "But they'll see us coming for sure, if they haven't already."

"The setup doesn't look like they're doing external observation, and I haven't seen any cameras, but you may be right," he admitted. "Give me a comm unit and I'll go in first, then signal you and your team to follow."

"By yourself?" the FBI agent asked, sounding incredulous. "I'm not going to be responsible for you getting yourself killed!"

"I don't have any intention of getting killed, but if we go in there guns blazing, it's not out of the question that they'll detonate the bomb. I'd like to go in quiet and fast. Once I've got a better idea of the situation, I'll signal you. As your team enters, I'll secure the bomb, if there is one."

Seles pursed his lips in thought, then nodded. "All right," he said. "But the second I hear shots or think you're in trouble, we're coming in anyway."

"Agreed," Bolan said. "Let's get going."

They moved to the back of the FBI agent's SUV, where Bolan took a comm unit and put it in his ear, then did a quick radio check. When it checked out, he said, "I'm going to need some bolt cutters for the fence." Seles found a pair in the kit in the back and handed them to him.

"Don't get dead while you're sneaking around in there," he said. "And don't be a hero. Just go in, spot for us and signal for the cavalry when you're in position, okay?"

"Okay," Bolan said, not bothering to explain to him that he only took orders from the President of the United States.

"Be fast, Cooper," Seles finished. "We're awfully exposed out here."

"I'll be fast. Just be ready when I signal," Bolan said, turning and jogging away from the man. He liked Seles, but the agent was starting to fold under the stress of the day's events. Seles's concerns, while understandable, wouldn't change the situation. And the fact that he'd shown up here with only three men told Bolan everything he needed to know about how stretched law enforcement of every stripe was in the city.

He reached the pedestrian gate and used the bolt cutters to snap through the padlock, which he removed and set quietly on the ground. Easing the gate open, he gritted his teeth at the not-very-quiet sound the hinges made. Leaving it open behind him, Bolan ran across the cracked blacktop of the parking lot and made it to the door, where he stopped.

The door itself wasn't anything special at first glance, but he didn't dare risk setting off an alarm at this point. He took the time to examine it more closely and saw nothing to indicate any kind of electronic alarm. Bolan removed an electronic device from an inner pocket of his field jacket—an electromagnetic lockpick. Inserting the slender extension into the door lock, he pushed the button on the side that would activate it, causing the metal of the pick to vibrate silently and force the tumblers into the release position.

He eased the door handle open when the lock clicked free, removed the device and returned it to the hidden pocket in his coat. Slipping inside, he pushed the door almost shut behind him. There was a short hall in front of him that led to another door—this one with a glass pane. On the wall to his right, an old-fashioned clock that employees would use to check in and out sat forgotten, its green metal sides slowly giving way to rust splotches.

Stepping silently up to the next door, Bolan peered through the glass and into the main warehouse. He quickly realized that the reason for the darkness of the building from the outside was that the terrorists had built an interior wall, sealing off all light. Even the windows were covered. In the center of the warehouse floor, a large cube made of Plexiglas or some other see-through material held a ball-shaped object made of a dull-colored metal. Holes had been cut into the glass and protective gloves attached, so that someone could work on the object inside the cube while remaining safe from it. Next to the cube, four men worked at two different tables covered with various bits of equipment, including a laptop computer.

All four carried sidearms, and he saw two assault rifles leaning against the table. From his present angle, Bolan couldn't see the catwalk above, but knew that the other two men were there. He'd expected more, considering the scope of the operation, but couldn't worry about that at the moment. What he was looking for in the dim light was which man was closest to the detonator. Unfortunately, he didn't see it.

He tapped the button to activate his comm unit. "This is Cooper. I'm inside. Confirming four men on the main floor of the warehouse and the presence of what appears to be a bomb of some kind."

Seles's voice replied in his ear. "Is it armed?"

"I can't tell from my current position. But it's obvious that a stealth approach is impossible."

"Stand by, Cooper," he said. "I'll be there in less than two minutes. Blue Team, move into ready position. We'll do a hard entry on my signal."

Another voice said, "Moving into position and standing by."

Shifting to see if he could spot the men on the catwalk, Bolan almost didn't notice the sentry who was staring at him in stunned surprise through the glass panel of the door.

"We're made," he said into his earpiece, then jumped sideways, sliding down to the floor as the sentry opened fire.

In the tiny hallway there was nowhere to hide, and since surprise and stealth were no longer options, he responded the only way he could. He drew the Desert Eagle and fired two quick shots through the bottom of the door at knee level.

The heavy slugs tore through the rotted wood and into the man's legs. He screamed and went down, his finger clutching the trigger of his assault rifle, which continued to spray bullets into the air.

"Here we go," Bolan said, slamming into the door with his shoulder as gunfire erupted from the back of the warehouse and Seles was shouting in his ear to wait for his team.

Waiting time was over. It was time for action. It was time for the Executioner.

12

What was left of the door crashed to the floor, landing on top of the screaming sentry. Bolan dove through the opening, then cut left, firing the Desert Eagle as he moved. His comm unit was going crazy, with both Seles and the men entering from the back of the building talking over each other. The four men in the middle of the warehouse had all armed themselves and were shooting wildly at the shadows around them.

Considering there wasn't much of anything for cover, Bolan went for what was available, which was a well-shadowed nook beneath the stairs leading to the catwalk above. He took careful aim at the man closest to the bomb, and dropped him with a well-placed round in the hip. The impact spun him in a complete circle, and he dropped his weapon as he clutched at the excruciatingly painful injury. The remaining men didn't seem to know where to focus their fire, and all three ran in opposite directions.

Seles came through the broken doorway where Bolan had entered, and didn't hesitate to put two rounds into the chest of the man running toward him. That left two men on the floor and one on the catwalk.

Bolan scanned the metal walkway above him and spotted the man trying to pry open the wood covering the window in an attempt to escape. He moved on catlike feet up the stairs as he heard the other two men go down in a hail of gunfire at the back of the building. The FBI men were obviously a little overzealous, so it was a good thing that he'd only injured the first two, so they had someone to question when it was over.

In his earpiece, he heard Seles say, "Stand down, everyone." A comment that Bolan himself ignored as he crept up behind the man frantically trying to escape through a window that was too small by about half. He was just a few feet behind him when some sense must have told the man that there was someone there.

The terrorist whipped around, trying to pull a cheap-looking 9 mm from his waistband. Bolan gunned him down without hesitation, the echoes from his shot loud in the relative silence of the warehouse. "*Now* everyone can stand down," he muttered into his comm unit.

"Round up the ones who are alive," Seles ordered, "and let's get an ambulance over here. Blue Team, I want a site report in two minutes."

Bolan left the terrorist on the catwalk for someone else to clean up and quickly made his way back down to the warehouse floor. Seles and one of his team members were standing next to the Plexiglas cube housing the bomb.

"What happened to 'quiet and fast'?" Seles asked as he approached. "And not being a hero?"

Bolan shrugged and offered a grin. "One of the guards up on the catwalk came down the steps and spotted me through the door. I decided it was better to act than get shot while I waited for the cavalry to arrive."

Seles smiled back. "Good choice, it seems."

"Sir," the man examining the bomb said, "my radioactivity detector is showing low-level amounts of uranium, which fits, considering that the bomb is inside that Plexiglas case. It's hot."

"Okay," Seles said. "It's not armed, is it?"

The man shook his head. "No. It doesn't look like they

were finished building it quite yet. I'll call the rest of the team in and we'll get it locked down."

"See to it," Seles replied, turning his attention back to Bolan. "This was excellent work, Cooper. I'll see to it you get a commendation in your file."

Bolan shook his head, his eyes looking at the bomb housing inside the case. "Save it," he said. "This isn't it."

Seles's face turned a rather ugly shade of red, bordering on purple, but he somehow controlled his voice when he said, "What do you mean, 'This isn't it'?"

"It's too easy," Bolan explained. "Six guys in a warehouse? The bomb sitting out in the open?"

"Oh, for God's sake, Cooper!" the FBI agent snarled. "Do you want to take on a whole army of terrorists or something?" The distant wail of an approaching ambulance accompanied his words.

"Listen, Denny, and think about it," he said. "The people running this were clever enough to smuggle uranium into the United States, start riots and a major fire to keep law enforcement distracted all over the city and not leave any significant trail behind them. Does it make sense that these six guys—the one upstairs looked like he was using a 9 mm that was bought in a pawn shop back in the sixties—are the ones behind this?"

Seles started to argue, then took a deep breath and stopped himself. Ignoring Bolan, he turned to the man who'd called in the bomb team. "Can you check out that bomb somehow? See if it's the real McCoy?" He grasped the man's shoulder and added, "*Without* accidentally setting it off?"

"Sure," he said. "They don't have it finished, like I said. There's no detonator in the main panel. I can pull off the housing cover and see what's beneath it."

"Do it."

Bolan and Seles watched as the man used the protective

gloves and the tools inside the Plexiglas case to slowly remove the housing cover. It took several minutes, but the last screw was removed, then he gently pried it open. Beneath, where the uranium rods should be, was an empty compartment.

"Nothing there, sir," the man said. "There was uranium here at one point, but the bomb itself is DOA."

"Son of a bitch!" Seles cried. "What a fucking waste of time!"

Bolan was reluctantly forced to agree. Once again, they'd been played and led by the nose—this time by his very own informant. "I'm sorry, Denny," he said. "We can only follow the leads we've got."

"So far, your leads have pretty much sucked, Cooper," the agent accused. "And everywhere you go, you leave a trail of bodies for me to clean up."

"I understand that this is a stressful situation, but taking it out on me isn't going to help," Bolan said quietly.

The agent sucked in a big breath, then sighed and said, "You know what, Cooper? You're absolutely right. Taking it out on you won't help. What *will* help is getting my ass back to the EOC and coming up with leads of my own that actually go somewhere."

Bolan contemplated arguing with the man, but decided against it. Seles was a good agent, but he was upset and the mounting pressure was getting to him. "If that's what you feel is best," he said.

"I do, Agent Cooper, and as far as I'm concerned, you're off the case," he added, pointing a finger in his direction. "Go back to chasing drug dealers or whatever it is you do when you're not wasting law-enforcement resources on wild-goose chases."

"That first one is free," the Executioner said, his voice dropping down to a low growl as his own patience frayed. "But if you point that finger at me again, I'm going to break it off and feed it to you, Denny." He stepped closer, ensuring that only Seles could hear him. "You don't have any authority over me or my involvement in this case. If you don't believe it, go back to the EOC and call the White House. In the meantime, I'm going to get back to work. All of this was a feint, just like the riots and the train explosion. They're playing us, but if that's the song you want to sing, I can't stop you."

His long speech seemed to take the FBI man by surprise, but he recovered quickly, nodded, and said, "Fuck you, Cooper. Now get off my scene."

"Good luck, Special Agent Seles," Bolan said, then turned and walked out of the warehouse. He needed to get back and question Imam Al-Qadir about his source, and if he found out that the imam was involved…well, he himself wasn't a very religious man, and he was certain he could find ways to inspire Al-Qadir to talk, even if they weren't spiritually based.

VINCENT WALKER'S FLIGHT got him on the ground in Detroit just after three o'clock in the morning. He was awake when the plane landed, and a car was already waiting for him when he stepped off the private jet. He'd changed clothing during the flight and presently wore a freshly pressed, black pinstriped suit, white shirt and red tie. Walker wasn't the kind of man to carry a briefcase—he could keep track of incredible amounts of information without referring to notes, and he possessed a nearly eidetic memory for details. Still, on this trip, he'd brought his own tablet computer, as well as his smartphone.

Less than thirty minutes later, the car pulled to a stop in front of the EOC. Walker didn't wait for the driver, but got out on his own. In the distance, he could see the glow from fires that were still burning from the train explosion, and farther off still, the sounds of sirens as police attempted to deal with the riots erupting along the 8 Mile Road region.

The early-morning air was crisp, and he took a deep breath, exhaled then went inside.

Allison Hart was waiting for him by the main desk. Under normal circumstances, Walker thought she was probably an attractive woman; at the moment, however, she looked exhausted. "Miss Hart," he said, extending a hand. "Deputy Director Vincent Walker, NSA."

She shook his hand. "Welcome to the Detroit EOC, Mr. Walker," she said. Even her voice sounded tired. "I understand why you're here and I'll do everything I can to support you."

Hart turned to the uniformed man at the desk. "Please give Mr. Walker a pass card." She waited until he'd set it up and done the initial swipe, then handed it to him. He put it in his suit pocket.

"Thank you," he said. "Let's get started, shall we?"

"Of course," she said. "Follow me, please. Denny Seles is waiting for us in my office. He's got an update from the field."

"Good news, I hope," Walker said, following her down the short hallway and into the main auditorium area. He ignored the eyes that turned his way, knowing there would be plenty of talk that the situation "wasn't fair." He had no interest in fair. Results were the name of the game to him.

"No, but it's not bad news, either. We thought we'd caught a break in the case, but it turned into a dead end. Yet another feint from whoever is running this terrorist group. This seems to be a well-organized effort on several fronts. Whoever is behind this is an expert at tapping our resources."

"Did it generate any additional leads?"

"I'll let Denny brief you," she said, as they reached the door to her office and stepped inside. "Deputy Director Walker, this is Special Agent in Charge Denny Seles."

The two men shook hands briefly, and Walker waved everyone to sit down. Once they were seated, he said, "Let's start by getting a couple of things clear. Allison, I have no intention of forcing you out—any more than I intend to replace Denny in the field. That said, everything *will* run through me. If there's new data, I want it. If you're chasing a lead, I want to know about it. Is that clear?"

Both of them nodded in weary acceptance, and he continued, "Agent Seles, I understand you have a briefing for me?"

"I do," Denny said, detailing the events of the night up to that point. "Of the six terrorists we found in the warehouse, four are dead and the other two are wounded. As soon as they've been treated, I've ordered them brought in for questioning."

Walker shook his head. "You aren't set up to take care of basic medical needs here?" he asked.

"No," Hart said. "We're an EOC, not a crime unit."

"Very well," he said. "But I want two agents with them at all times. In the meantime, Agent Seles, I want you and your men back out in the train yards. That seems like the best jumping-off point."

"I'm not sure I follow you," he said. "It's nothing more than a feint."

"Feint or no, if there's any chance of missed evidence—and I wouldn't be surprised if there were—it's the best place we've got to find it. The warehouse is going to be a washout. That was a setup from the beginning, but it's possible that they accidentally left a clue in the train yard. Go back and sweep it again. All of it."

Seles shrugged. "I got the orders out of Washington, too, so it's your show." He got to his feet. "But you aren't in my food chain, Mr. Walker, so I want it on the record that I think this is a waste of time. We've gained everything that we're going to from the train yard. I don't have time to retrace steps."

"Noted, Agent Seles," he said. "But let's be perfectly clear. I may not be in your food chain, but if you fuck with me, I can make sure you spend the rest of your life running the field office in Bumfuck, Alaska. Are we understanding each other?"

"Perfectly," Seles answered.

"One last thing," Walker said. "In the initial reports, there was mention of this DEA agent Matt Cooper who's been working in the field. I want him in here for a full debrief immediately."

"I'll let him know," Seles said, "but I don't think you'll enjoy it."

"Why's that?"

Seles laughed coldly. "Because he's even more dangerous than you are and about half as cooperative. He seems to operate from his own playbook. "

Walker thought that highly unlikely and just said, "Get him in here. And Ms. Hart, I'll want section reports from your departments in ten minutes. Let's set it up in the main conference room."

"I'll see to it," she said.

"That will be all," he added, dismissing them. Things were moving in the right direction—he'd established himself at the top of the chain. These people would step in line with minimal grumbling like the good little soldiers that they were. All he had to do was catch the people behind this madness to secure his place at the table permanently.

SELES PULLED HART ASIDE in the hallway. His blood was boiling from the high-handed treatment by Walker. He wondered who this guy thought he was that he could order him or his team around. He could see that Hart was just as rattled.

"Have you been able to dig up anything on this guy?" Seles asked.

"No, not yet, but I have a man I know working on it. I can't believe they sent him in here, like we don't already have enough problems."

"Look, I'm going to send some people over to the train yards to finish looking around, but we're not going to find anything. In the meantime, I'm going to keep my people working the real problem."

"How do you plan to do that with this guy breathing down our necks?"

"I don't know, but I'll figure something out."

13

"*Assalamu alaikum,* my friend," Imam Al-Qadir said when Bolan entered his office. "You have good news?"

The Executioner didn't know if the imam had been misled or was part of the group that was orchestrating the events of this long night. All he knew for sure was that he was tired of dancing like a marionette on a string, and the information that had led them to yet another dead end had come from the imam. "There is no peace tonight," he said. "And the only good news is that I'm still looking for the people behind this."

The soft glow from the lamp on the imam's desk cast soft shadows on the holy man's face. Bolan watched several different expressions chase each other across his features and knew this was a man in turmoil, and that there was information he still had that might prove useful. He needed answers, he needed them immediately and he knew how to get them.

"My friend," he said, pitching his voice low and soft, "I think you need to tell me how to find the source of your information. Who told you about the warehouse?"

"You know I cannot do that," he said. "I would be breaking the sanctity of the mosque!"

"That was already broken when you gave me information that was a set-up," Bolan replied. "So either you knew it was a set-up—in which case, you're a part of this—or you didn't,

and the person who gave this information to you was purpose-
fully trying to use your office to protect himself. Which is it?"

The imam dropped to his knees, crying out in prayer.
Bolan knelt next to him and placed a hand on his shoulder.
"I am not accusing you, Imam Al-Qadir. I am *asking* you to
help me put a stop to this before it goes any further. Surely
Allah would approve of ending this violence before even more
people die." The imam shuddered beneath Bolan's hand.

"I did not intentionally deceive you," the imam said. His
voice was barely audible, a mere whisper.

"I can accept that you were deceived yourself," Bolan replied. "Now you must tell me where to find the man who gave
you this information."

"I cannot—must not—break the sanctity of the mosque."

"There's no sanctity in a lie. People *died* tonight because
of that lie, Imam. More people will die before this is over.
Help me protect as many as I can and bring the real evil to
justice tonight."

The imam rose to his feet and Bolan moved with him. "If
I tell you this information, I may become a target of these
very people. The extremists in our faith do not understand
Allah's mercy, do not seek out His peace."

"Extremists of any flavor never do," the Executioner said.
"That's why the world needs people like me to stop them."

Al-Qadir walked over to his desk. Pulling out a pad of
paper, he began to write, then paused in mid-stroke. "This
man…he could simply be a pawn in this wicked game. Will
you treat him fairly?"

"As fairly as I can," he said. "My job tonight is to find the
people behind all this and save lives. To bring an end to this
terror. Right now, this very stretch of road belongs to those
who intend to harm hundreds, maybe thousands of people.
I'll do my best to be fair, but not at the price of other lives.

If that means taking one, evening the odds even a little, then that's what I'll do."

"Causing the death of another is never the answer, my friend."

Bolan offered a slight shrug. "Protecting those who would cause death isn't the answer, either. You know that or you wouldn't be helping me, you'd be helping them. The people you have vowed to serve are being hurt by all of this, and it's your duty as much as it is mine to make sure that they are protected."

The imam pondered his words for a moment, then finished writing the name and address and handed it to Bolan.

"I pray to Allah that I am doing the right thing and I will pray that you do the right things, as well. Even someone like you must serve Allah's purpose."

"I do what needs to be done and I guess that will have to be enough for Allah and everyone else," he replied. Then Bolan turned and left the mosque. The imam was a good man, but Bolan had little use for someone who would protect a terrorist at the expense of innocent lives. Hopefully, the holy man would come to peace with his choice and maybe even be a better man for doing the right thing for the world, even if it was the wrong thing in the eyes of his god.

After all, so far as the Executioner knew, Allah didn't live in Detroit.

DRIVING AWAY FROM the mosque, Bolan hit a stoplight and entered his destination address into the GPS unit on his dash. Several blocks down the street, he could see fires burning and the telltale lights of police cars and fire trucks—he only hoped he wouldn't have to go through that to get to where he was going. The night had been long enough without taking detours through rioting gangs. As the light turned green, his cell phone rang and he saw Seles's number on the display.

"I thought you were done with me?" Bolan asked when he answered the call.

"I thought I was, but I'm not calling for me, so I guess that works out."

Bolan kept his silence, glancing at the GPS unit and hooking a left a full block before he'd have been forced to turn around.

"Anyway," Seles continued when Bolan didn't say anything, "Washington sent out someone to take over the situation here. I'm calling for him."

"What are you talking about?" Bolan asked. "From what I could tell, Allison seems to be doing a pretty good job."

"I thought so, too, but apparently, they think us yokels need to be shown how to run things. The new guy is NSA, name of Vincent Walker. He walked in here with a hard-on and it's getting bigger by the minute. You know him?"

"One of those, huh?" Bolan said. "I don't know him, but I know his type well enough."

"Well, you'll be happy to hear he has set his sights on you. He wants you to come in to the EOC and debrief."

"Not so much happy as vaguely annoyed," he said. "It's lucky for me that I don't answer to him."

Bolan could hear Denny chuckling on the other end. "You know you're likely to catch hell when it all comes out in the wash."

"Maybe, maybe not. What I do know is that I don't have time to answer a bunch of useless questions from some bureaucrat. I'm above his pay grade whether he likes it or not."

"I'm not telling him that!" Seles said.

"Then I'll tell him myself. Put me through to him."

Bolan waited on hold as he continued to maneuver through the streets to the house of Abdul Batin, the name the imam had given him. He parked half a block down, and was using his night-vision-capable binoculars to scope out the house when Walker came on the line.

"What is this about you not coming in for a debrief, Agent Cooper?" he said, skipping right over any preliminaries or pleasantries.

"I don't have time for it right now," Bolan said. "I'm on a trail."

"You've got balls, Cooper, I'll give you that. But when I say come in for a debrief that's what I mean. Now get your ass back to the EOC."

"Listen to me, Walker, and pay attention. There is only one way this is going to go and it's my way. I don't know what authority you think you have over me, because you don't have any. I will continue to feed the information I find as I uncover it, but I don't work for you."

"This is supposed to be a joint task force…" Walker started to say, but Bolan cut him off.

"I'm not part of any task force. While you sit around the EOC and make everyone miserable, I'm going to be doing my job. I suggest you leave me to it, and I'll leave you to yours. I'll contact you when I have more information."

Bolan hit the end button on his cell phone, cutting off the call. It began to ring again immediately, but he hit Ignore and turned it to Vibrate. He had more important things to do than satisfy the power-hungry urges of a Washington bureaucrat.

WALKER SLAMMED THE PHONE DOWN so hard it actually hurt his hand. It had been a long time since anyone had spoken to him that way, and as far as he was concerned, hell itself would freeze over before it ever happened again. He punched Matt Cooper's information into his computer.

"The prick might think he can get away from me, but wait until I have his superiors hand me his balls for breakfast," he muttered to himself.

The file loaded briefly, but before he could read more than a name, the file went blank and a message popped on screen: ACCESS DENIED.

"What?" Walker said. "Unbelievable." He backtracked to the main screen, then typed in what the NSA called an Alpha Code—it was a top-level clearance code that would give him access to virtually anything in the federal databases, except the nuclear launch codes. He typed in Cooper's name once more, and again, his file loaded just a name. The rest of the fields were blank, then a new message popped up: TS/SCI/PEO. ACCESS DENIED.

He'd never seen such a designation before. Shaking his head in disbelief at his inability to bring up the DEA agent's file, he tried one more time, and failed again. Walker pushed back from the desk, then used the intercom built into the phone to call Seles into his office. The FBI agent stepped inside within a couple of minutes.

"I was just about to leave," he said. "What can I do for you?"

"I want you to track down Agent Cooper and I want him arrested."

"On what grounds?" Seles asked. "Last I knew, he was an officer of the law, not a law-breaker."

"Are you questioning my authority?" Walker asked.

Seles shook his head. "Not at all, but if you're having me arrest someone I need to know the charge."

"The charge is espionage."

"You're joking, right?" Seles asked. "I don't understand."

"I never joke, Agent Seles, and you don't have to understand. Now, ping his phone for coordinates, track him down and take him into custody. This isn't your show to run anymore and you will obey my orders or you can get the hell out of my investigation."

Seles turned to leave, still shaking his head.

"And Agent Seles," Walker said, "if you come back here without him, I'm going to assume that you're part of whatever he's up to. And then I'm coming after you."

The man didn't reply, but simply let the door shut behind him. Walker turned back to the computer screen to stare at the security message again: TS/SCI/PEO. In all his years of government service, he'd never seen it before. Not one time.

The common denominator in every "near miss" tonight in trying to catch the terrorists was Matt Cooper. Perhaps it was because he wasn't a federal agent at all, but a plant, or some kind of double agent. Either way, he'd have some answers and soon.

It was the only thing that made any real sense. As a Deputy Director for the NSA, Walker had access to the highest levels of intelligence in the government. If a simple personnel file had been sealed off, then something—or someone—wasn't right.

Until he found out what or who, everyone was a potential suspect, but he had a feeling that it all started and ended with this Matt Cooper. As soon as Seles brought him in, Walker knew at least a hundred ways to make a man like that spill his guts. He'd pry his secrets out of him and find the trail that everyone else had overlooked.

All of this Detroit mess would be over by sunrise, and he'd be on his way to the top.

14

The house, a small once-white bungalow in need of a fresh coat of paint, regular trash service and an owner that knew something about hedge-trimming, appeared quiet as Bolan approached. The sun would be coming up soon, but for the time being, the darkness held, and that served his purposes as he slipped up the driveway and around the back of the house. The door there was also dark and he looked carefully for any sign of motion lights before he moved in closer.

He tested the door and found it locked, but used his tool to pick it silently. Bolan eased the door open and stepped inside, shutting it just as quietly as he'd opened it. The back door led to the kitchen, and he was surprised to see that the room was spotlessly clean. The inside of the house didn't match what the outside had led him to expect. He'd imagined wading through cockroaches and mounds of unwashed dishes. A couple of plates and some cheap silverware were drying in the dish rack.

On cat's feet, he moved past the kitchen, peering into the dark, empty living room, before turning and moving down the hall. Light pooled through the crack at the base of one door. Bolan leaned closer and listened. A television was on, though the volume was turned low. A faint rustling of paper, but no conversation. Batin was alone.

Bolan leaned back and lashed out with one boot, kicking

in the door. Batin was sitting at a desk. He yanked open a drawer, sticking a hand inside, as the Executioner drew the Desert Eagle from his shoulder rig.

"If you want to live, you'd better get your hands where I can see them."

The Desert Eagle was a large, intimidating weapon. Batin slowly withdrew his hand from the drawer, placing it with his other on top of the desk. Bolan moved forward and placed the muzzle of his weapon on the man's forehead.

"You are Abdul Batin?"

The man offered a very small nod of his head.

"Good. You and I are going to have a talk. You are going to answer my questions, and I will let you live. If you don't, then this is going to be the longest night of your life. Nod if you understand."

Small beads of sweat were breaking on Batin's nodding forehead, and Bolan lowered his weapon. Like the kitchen, this room was meticulously clean. There was a laptop computer on the desk, several pieces of paper, and a suitcase on the bed. He looked more closely and saw that one of the sheets of paper was an itinerary for a flight leaving out of Detroit in a few hours.

"Planning a trip?" he asked.

"To visit family in California," Batin said.

Bolan picked up the sheet of paper. "This was purchased less than an hour ago," he said. "People don't usually buy their tickets at the last minute."

"Family emergency," he said, clipping his words. His eyes hadn't yet left the muzzle of the Desert Eagle.

"More like an impending emergency here," Bolan snapped. "Now, who's behind the bomb we found tonight...or should I say, the decoy?"

"I don't know what you're talking about," Batin said, his words heavily accented by both his culture and his fear.

Without any warning, Bolan flipped the pistol around in his hand and smashed the butt onto the top of Batin's hand. Bones cracked with the force of the blow. Batin cried out and reflexively cradled the hand against his chest as he rocked back and forth.

"See, things were going so well. I was asking questions, you were telling me lies, but there was communication. Then, you had to pull out the old 'I don't know what you're talking about' line. We both know you do."

Batin kept his silence, and Bolan had to admire the man's resolve. Sadly, things hadn't even gotten harsh yet.

"Listen to me carefully, Batin," he said. "Under normal circumstances, I'd have more time to play games with you. I'd ask nicely and we'd spend some real time getting the answers out of you. But the way this night has gone, I suspect I don't have much time at all."

He waited to see if Batin responded, and when he didn't, Bolan continued. "You're in a real hurry to leave town, Batin, which makes me think that I should drop you in the nearest cell downtown. Once that bomb is about to go off, you'll talk. You'll sing opera if it means saving your own life. But I can't take the chance that something would happen to you. So, I'm going to ask one more time. And either you answer me— truthfully—or I'm going to take you apart a piece at a time."

Bolan pressed the Desert Eagle into the man's left elbow. "I'll start by blowing off your arm, Batin. Now, who is behind this? Who am I looking for?"

"Yasim, Malick Yasim," Batin stammered. "He told me I would be helping the cause if I gave the information to the imam, but I don't know anything else!"

"Sure you do," Bolan said, "but we'll get to that in a minute." He stepped back and pulled out his handheld, hitting the button that would autodial Brognola on a secure line. Before the call could go through, the sound of the front door bursting open, followed by loud voices, stopped him. He hit the end button and slipped the device back into his coat.

In the small house, options were limited, so Bolan stepped to one side of the door frame, ready to take out the first person who stuck his head in the room. The voices moved down the hallway, calling out "Clear," and he realized that it was law enforcement. He was sliding the Desert Eagle back into its holster when Seles stuck his head into the room, training his own Glock on Bolan.

"If you came to help, Seles, I think you're a little late," he said.

"Put your hands up, Cooper. I'm placing you under arrest."

A bit stunned, Bolan cocked an eyebrow. "Aren't we supposed to be tracking down terrorists instead of arresting each other?"

"I'm here to take you back in to the EOC, Cooper. You're to be debriefed and possibly charged with espionage."

Walker was flexing his muscles, Bolan realized, but there was no way that Seles could know that. "What the hell are you talking about?"

"I have my orders."

"From Walker," he replied. "You aren't seriously going to let someone come in and derail us during this mess are you?"

"Just take out your gun and put it on the desk, nice and slow."

Bolan removed the Desert Eagle from his holster, then set it lightly on the desk, out of Batin's easy reach, and held up his hands. "Just bring this guy along with you, too. He's a material witness and was the one who flipped on the warehouse. I've already gotten a name from him."

Batin jumped to his feet and began yelling. "I don't know what he's talking about! This maniac breaks into my house and smashes my hand! I want my lawyer and medical attention. I will sue this whole city."

Seles stepped forward and looked at Batin's hand, which was already swollen and turning terrific shades of dark blue and purple.

"Christ, Cooper, what did you do to him?" He turned the officer behind him. "Have this man cleared by the paramedics before we take him back to the EOC and then give us the room."

The officers pulled Batin along with them as he loudly protested his treatment. Seles holstered his weapon and walked up to Bolan.

"I don't know what in the hell is going on here, Cooper, but Walker wants you brought in. You've been lone-wolfing it all night, and he seems to think you're the reason we've been running in circles. I need to know right now if you've been playing us. Are you some kind of spy for them?"

"Denny," Bolan said, "if I were a spy, I'd have helped them kill you at the warehouse. You'd be dead. This is just Walker trying to flex his muscles because I wouldn't do what he wanted. He's trying to be a hero and make himself look good."

Seles sighed heavily, and rubbed his hands over his face. He looked tired, but at this point, Bolan figured they all did. Everything they'd found so far had been one dead end after another, but if he could give Brognola the name he'd gotten out of Batin, maybe they'd have something solid to start with. He started to say this to Seles when several gunshots rang out in the living room, ridiculously loud in the small space of the bungalow.

Seles drew his Glock and Bolan grabbed for his Desert Eagle without thinking that the FBI agent might not approve. He gave Bolan a quick glance, nodded, then the two of them went down the hallway.

The two officers who had been escorting Batin were lying on the living-room floor, while paramedics worked feverishly to stem the flow of blood from their wounds. Both had been shot at nearly point-blank range and it didn't look good.

"What the hell happened?" Seles yelled.

One of his team members who'd been stationed at the front door explained, "The suspect had a gun hidden. He waited until he could use the paramedic as a shield, then shot Johnson and Parker. He was out the back door so fast…" He shrugged. "We didn't give chase because we weren't clear on his status and there were Johnson and Parker to think about."

"Damn it!" Bolan cried. "Now all we've got is a name and nowhere to look for it!"

"Clear down the scene," Seles ordered, "then return to the EOC. We'll meet you there."

"You're still taking me in?" he asked, incredulously.

"No, but you're coming in all the same. Let's get Walker out of our hair and figure out what's next."

"I had what was next and you and Walker blew it. Let's go and get this done."

THE CORPORATE OFFICES OF AJ Engineering and Manufacturing were of no interest to Yasim, but they were part of a carefully designed industrial park. The outer line of buildings was offices, while behind them were storage facilities and warehouses. Access to the office buildings was simple—they faced the street and had public parking—but getting to the storage buildings was a bit more difficult. The grounds were fenced off with a twelve-foot-tall chain-link electrified fence topped with coiled barbed wire. Automatic motion lights and an active foot-patrol security presence ensured that getting close without being seen was virtually impossible. No reasonable expense had been spared, but the facilities were used to store very expensive materials ranging from computer components for the defense industry to the detonator that he needed to acquire in order to complete the bomb.

The bridge-wire detonator was small, but used gold and platinum components. Individually, it would be worth a small sum, but a large stockpile of them, stripped down for their valuable metal, would be worth a fortune. The company that made them, AJ Engineering and Manufacturing, was a supplier for large commercial mining operations all over the world that used the detonators for blasting. Fortunately, while the security systems in place here were formidable, they were less concerned with the people who worked for them.

Yasim had spent three months working nights as a temporary security guard to gain the information he would need to access the facility successfully and steal the detonator Sayf required.

Reaching the first exterior gate, Yasim pulled the unmarked cargo van to a stop and rolled down the window. The illuminated keypad glowed a soft green as he punched in the code he'd stolen from the security-office computer—he hoped that it was still valid. The code was thirteen digits in length, and the upside—if it worked—would be an invisible entry. The downside was that an invalid code would automatically alert the system, locking down the gate and sending a notification of a breach in progress to both security guards and the local police.

The memorized code processed silently for several seconds, then the screen flashed all green. Their endeavor obviously had Allah's blessing as the steel gates unlocked and began sliding back on their tracks, granting them access to the storage facilities.

Yasim and his men rolled into the compound in the unmarked van and used the same code to gain entry into the designated warehouse. Everything was laid out perfectly. In Yasim's opinion, the reason that so many so-called terrorist operations failed was lack of operational planning. Sayf had spent several years planning for this night, and his patience and trust in Yasim was paying off. Law enforcement, both local and federal, was distracted—busy following emergencies or false trails. Every step had been planned, with contingencies for the unexpected. The sunrise would see them almost finished with the weapon, and on this day they would succeed where so many others had failed.

The men quickly loaded three of the detonators—one for the actual weapon, and two for backup. As they prepared to leave, Yasim saw the tell-tale flicker of a flashlight moving toward them—one of the security guards on foot patrol. Undoubtedly, their presence would raise questions and they wouldn't be able to leave before the guard reached them.

Yasim hissed an order and waved his men into the van, then slid back into the shadows of the building. The security guard's eyes widened in surprise as he saw the van, and his hands were shaking as he slowly removed his gun from its holster and pointed it at the driver's-side window. "What are you doing here this late?" the man asked.

Yasim's men cooperated, smiling and talking to the guard to keep his attention focused on the van. Tucking in behind him, the man known as the Mummy slipped a thin, long blade from his sleeve. The razor-sharp blade offered a touch like a delicate pair of lips—so soft that in the first millisecond the guard may have thought he'd experienced a sense memory or perhaps a very faint breath of wind. His carotid artery fountained with the beats of his heart and he turned his stunned gaze to his attacker.

"Shh," Yasim said, glorying in the kill, even as he jabbed forward once more, this time puncturing the guard's larynx and preventing him from crying out.

The guard slumped to the ground, unconscious in seconds, and when he was dead, Yasim dragged the body into the storage unit. Perhaps the other security people would think he'd left or quit. It might be several days before the body was found, and by then it wouldn't matter in the least.

Wiping the blade clean, Yasim returned it to the hidden sheath in his sleeve, then closed the doors and locked them. Returning to the driver's seat of the van, he smiled. His work here was done and Sayf would be very pleased.

15

"You know this isn't right."

Bolan caught Seles's gaze in the mirror from the backseat of the black SUV. There was nothing more infuriating than being detained in the middle of a mission, but leaving Seles in the middle would only make things worse and Bolan was beginning to savor the idea of meeting Walker in person. Seles had insisted on making it look the way Walker would expect—and the Executioner was playing along. Seles had asked Bolan to turn over his gun and his phone, but he hadn't gone so far as handcuffing him.

"Denny, I need to make a call before we get to the EOC."

"To whom?" Seles asked.

Bolan considered the question and how best to answer, then said, "For the sake of this mission, we'll say my boss. The relationship is a little more complicated than that, but let's keep it simple."

"Fine," he said, passing Bolan's phone over the seat. "Just don't make me regret it."

Bolan laughed grimly and shook his head. "*You* won't, but Walker probably will," he said, punching in the code that would dial Brognola's secure line.

The man answered on the second ring, skipping the preamble. "I sincerely hope you're calling with good news, Striker. I've got a bunch of antsy people breathing down my neck."

"I wish that were the case, Hal. Instead of chasing down the bad guys, I've been arrested."

"What!" Brognola wasn't the kind of man to raise his voice, but this news caught him off guard. "On what charge?" he demanded.

"Apparently, espionage," Bolan said. "Washington sent out some NSA guy, Deputy Director Vincent Walker, to take over the operation. He thinks I'm playing for the other team for some reason and has had Denny Seles arrest me. He's taken a bad situation and made it into a farcical mess."

Brognola mumbled something under his breath, and Bolan said, "Pardon me?"

"I said 'power-hungry little prick,'" he replied, enunciating each word carefully. "This is ridiculous! I'll make a call and have this taken care of by the time you get there. The White House orders—and I'm looking at a copy—specified non-interference with both active and undercover field personnel. I'm sorry about this, Striker. I don't think the White House knows what he's up to out there, but I'll involve the President personally."

"Thanks, Hal. Oh, one more thing, do some digging on the name *Malick Yasim*. It was the name I got before my informant was allowed to escape."

"What do you mean *allowed*?" Hal asked, his voice dropping into a lower register that to anyone who knew him would be a loudly ringing alarm bell.

"I mean I was questioning him when Seles showed up to arrest me. While the suspect was receiving medical treatment he pulled a gun, shot two people and escaped. He was gone before I was even in the room with him again."

"You've got to be kidding me," Brognola said. "I'll have this Walker's ass before the day's even started. Hang tight and I'll get back to you with an update and whatever we've got on that name." The line went dead and Bolan reclined back into the plush leather of the seat and closed his eyes.

"What did your boss say?" Seles asked. "And for that matter, who is your boss?"

Choosing to ignore the second question, Bolan asked one of his own. "What would you say if one of your agents was arrested in the middle of an interrogation, then the suspect he was questioning shoots two officers and escapes, while the leads are getting cold as he's being transported in for a 'debriefing'?"

The hint of glee in Seles's voice was unmistakable. "*Someone* is getting hell."

"Bingo."

THE MINUTE WALKER'S SHOES hit the floor of the main auditorium inside the EOC, the area quieted. He felt a surge of personal satisfaction as the ants scurried to do his bidding, while keeping their heads down. Since taking command, he'd required each department lead to give an update every thirty minutes—or less, if information was urgent. His smartphone buzzed with an incoming text message and if anyone was watching when he read it they'd have seen an expression of what could only be described as terrifying joy cross his features. The message was from Seles: *Cooper in custody. ETA to EOC 10 minutes.* Pleased, Walker turned his attention to the running man approaching him.

"Excuse me, sir," he said.

"What is it?"

"Sir, there's a priority call from the White House. It's on a secure line in the Comm Room."

"I'll be right there," Walker said, privately perplexed. Why would anyone in the White House call him on a secure line that had to be routed into the Comm Room instead of just contacting him directly? It must be a highly sensitive matter, he thought, to require that level of privacy. He worked his way through the various groups of people in the auditorium, reaching the frosted-glass walls of the room. He stepped inside to find Hart waiting for him with the phone in her hand.

Angered, he stared at her, but found her gaze to be unblinking. "What the hell are you doing answering *my* call from the White House, Ms. Hart?"

"They asked to speak to me first," she said.

"I'll deal with you later," he said, holding out his hand for the handset, wondering what trouble she'd managed to cause.

"Mr. Walker, would you like to explain to me what in the blue hell you're doing down there?" the President of the United States snarled into the line.

Stunned, Walker stammered before saying, "Sir, I don't know what Ms. Hart has told you, but...everything, sir, everything here is well in hand."

"Ms. Hart didn't call me, I called her when I heard that instead of tracking down the terrorists, you're using Denny Seles and his field team to arrest an agent I personally assigned to this operation." The President was very angry—and that said something since he was generally a very patient man, given more to thoughtfulness and consideration than emotional displays. This wasn't good at all.

That son of a bitch Cooper, Walker thought. How was it possible that some field agent who didn't even have a visible file had access to the President? "I'm not sure I understand, sir. Agent Cooper—"

"Is acting under direct orders from me," the President interrupted with a low growl.

"I didn't...I didn't know that, sir. I was going over personnel files, and when I checked his, there were some things that didn't add up. I've never even seen a clearance like the one he has! If I could just speak with his supervisor..."

"You're speaking with his supervisor! He has *my* clearance. What do you think the PEO line is for? It's *Presidential Eyes Only.* Do you have any further questions about his authority or qualifications?"

"No, sir," Walker said, inwardly seething. He didn't understand how one field agent could have that much power.

"Then I can expect that he will be released and you will restrain yourself *to the letter* of your orders?"

"Yes, sir," he said. "Of course, sir. I was only trying to…"

"And let me be clear with you, Walker. If Agent Cooper yells 'frog,' you'll ribbit and jump, is that clear?"

This was as humiliating as anything he'd ever experienced—and as far as Walker was concerned, it was all Cooper's fault. "Yes, sir," he said, the words somehow getting past his clenched teeth.

"Get back to it," the President said, before slamming down the phone and severing the connection. Walker stared blankly at the phone in his hand, trying to collect himself. He glared again at Hart who looked at him with a composed expression, but she couldn't hide what was in her eyes. She was *enjoying* his humiliation. It didn't matter, he thought. When his approach got results and the terrorists were caught, this little slip would be forgotten in the bigger picture…and Matt Cooper would be nothing more than a bug on his windshield.

He put the phone back in the cradle. "When Seles and Cooper get here I want to see them both immediately."

"Yes, sir." Her voice was chipper. "Do you want me to call in advance and let them know that Cooper is to be released?"

"That won't be necessary, Ms. Hart. I'll handle it when they arrive." Spinning on his heels, Walker stalked out into the hallway toward the break room. He'd have a cup of coffee and wait for Seles and Cooper to arrive and clear everything up to the President's satisfaction.

Walker twisted the pen in his hand until it cracked from the tension. He shoved past several people until the hallway began parting like the Red Sea. Just ahead of him and down one level in the terraced auditorium, he saw two people enter the room. The first man was one of the uniformed security guards; the second was a rather nondescript-looking man wearing a trench coat.

The security guard's hands were raised and his face was a pasty-white color with the exception of his cheeks, which showed two hectic spots of red so bright that they looked like clown makeup. Time slowed down and Walker instantly knew they were in trouble. His feelings of shame at the President's call dropped away and his vision narrowed to the two men slowly moving into the auditorium. Perhaps he could stop whatever was about to happen.

He moved down to intercept them, then held out a hand. "Stop!" he said. "Don't move!"

The security guard's eyes widened in an odd combination of desperation and hope, yet he was shaking his head back and forth so rapidly that his ears could've passed for a hummingbird's wings. "Bomb…bomb…bomb…" he stuttered.

Walker turned his gaze on the man behind the security guard. He was sweating profusely, but he didn't *look* like a terrorist. He had blond hair and blue eyes—he couldn't have been a day over twenty-one, Walker thought. He looked like any other kid on the street, maybe just going to community college or working a job and figuring out his life. American kids weren't terrorists.

Walker held up his hands again. "Just stop, okay? Let's talk about this."

The kid pulled open his trench coat, letting it drop to the floor, as he muttered incoherently to himself. Beneath the coat, he wore a sweat-soaked white prayer shirt Walker recognized as a kurta. Over that, a heavy black vest was encircled by a ring of C-4.

The sight of the bomb stole Walker's tongue and with his

hands still raised, he began to back away slowly. The kid moved toward him and his words began to come more clearly. *"Masha'Allah."* It meant *praise,* but the literal translation was "Whatever Allah wills."

People in the EOC had begun to notice what was happening. Time slowed even further. A woman screamed, and the wild thought passed through Walker's mind that it was Hart. He continued to back away, but now the kid was coming closer, moving faster.

"Masha'Allah! Masha'Allah! Masha'Allah!"

Running backward, unable to tear his eyes away from his assailant, Walker wondered how this could have happened. How could this kid, this American kid, be in his EOC with a bomb vest? How did he get inside?

Tripping, Walker fell just as the madman reached him, his words a strong, rhythmic chant. *"Masha'Allah!"* he finished, pushing the button in his clenched fist.

The moment stretched out like salt-water taffy, and Walker realized that the room was perfectly silent. Then the bomb exploded, the world went red, then white and, finally, dark.

16

"Good God!" Seles yelled, slamming on the brakes. Just as they'd pulled into the parking lot of the EOC the building had exploded. Portions of it were in the parking spaces, while most of the structure looked as if it had collapsed in on itself.

"Back up, Denny," Bolan snapped from the backseat. When he hesitated, the Executioner leaned over the seat, grabbed the transmission lever and shoved it into Reverse. "Back up!"

Seles hit the gas and the tires squealed on the damp pavement as the big SUV lurched backward. Debris from the building rained down into the lot. Wood, metal and—Bolan noted with a clinical eye—body parts. Once they were in the clear, Seles stopped the SUV once more and both men jumped out.

"Let's go," Bolan said, setting off across the street at a jog.

Fire trucks began to roll onto the scene, which wasn't surprising considering that the station was only half a block away—and everyone was on duty. Bolan maneuvered around them and made his way into what was left of the building. Running to the raggedy edge of the wreckage, both men began helping people who were making their way out of the rubble. Paramedics and firefighters worked to get them into the parking lot where emergency workers were doing triage and shipping the most seriously injured off to hospitals. When the mass exodus ended, Bolan and Seles looked at each other.

Their faces were black with soot, and their clothing spattered with wet ash. The fire from the explosion hadn't taken long to put out, but there was still plenty of evidence floating in the cold air. As the sun cleared the horizon, a silent communication passed between the two men. It was time to go in.

"Hey, you can't go in there! The whole building could come down!" the Fire Chief yelled as they started to work their way forward.

"Shut up, Chief," Seles snapped, "and get some men over here to help us start looking for people."

Bolan and Seles began to search for survivors. The building that had once been a model of efficient operations, with a multilevel auditorium, glass-walled offices and an information flow designed to handle everything from fires to snowstorms to major law-enforcement situations, now resembled a doughnut with a bite taken out of it. The explosion had funneled down the main hallway, blowing out the doors and collapsing the auditorium into piles of rubble. Small spaces made crawling through the debris a challenge, especially as live wires that had been embedded in the walls and the ceiling were sparking on the floor. Bolan reached one of the fire boxes on the wall and pulled the ax free, while Seles used his radio to tell the Fire Chief to have the power company shut down the entire grid for this block.

Using the ax to shove the worst of the debris out of the way, they worked forward, the point of a human chain of firefighters and paramedics, looking for survivors in the early light of the day. Sadly, they were finding more bodies than living people, and Bolan kept a running count in his head. So far, he'd counted twenty-eight dead, but he suspected the toll was far worse than that. According to Seles, there had been at least two hundred people in the building when the explosion occurred.

They reached the auditorium area, and early morning sky was visible through the smoke curling above them. A large pile of debris, mostly drywall covered by girders, blocked their path.

"This will be the worst of it," Seles said. "Everyone worked in here."

Bolan kept his silence, his anger at the situation turning inward and growing more and more focused.

"Help! Is someone there? Help me!" a weak voice called from the pile of debris. Bolan moved forward, and together with Seles, started carefully moving the rubble that blocked their way into the auditorium.

"Hang on!" Seles said. "We've got to be cautious uncovering you."

Bit by bit, they cleared everything away, finally revealing the battered form of Allison Hart. A long, thin cut streaked one cheek, and her clothing was burned in several places. They reached out and gently lifted her to her feet. Bolan noted that she was going to have one hell of a shiner on her left eye.

"Are you okay?" he asked, surveying her for other injuries as she allowed herself to be held by Seles while she collected herself.

"I'll be all right," she said, swiping at the blood trickling down her cheek. She swayed a bit on her feet and Seles tightened his grasp on her. "Sorry," she said. "I'm a bit woozy. When the ceiling came down, I got conked on the head."

"Let's get you checked out," Bolan said. "Denny, do you want to take her to the ambulance? I'll stay here and help them clear debris so we can get farther into the auditorium."

Hart shook her head, took a deep breath and said, "No. No ambulance. Right now, we need to regroup."

"That cut looks like it might need a stitch or ten," Seles suggested cautiously.

"Then I'll get it stitched and we keep going," she snapped. "When that maniac started running after Walker, I realized that we've been going about this all wrong. I was trying to get behind him when he blew himself up, which is how I ended up here, instead of being right next to him."

"What maniac?" Seles asked.

"There was a terrorist with a bomb vest," she said. "He came in here, shouting, and blew himself and the building to pieces."

"Middle Eastern?" he asked.

She shook her head, as a paramedic appeared and handed her a clean bandage for her face. "American kid," she replied. "Can you believe it?"

"What happened to Walker?" Bolan asked.

"He's dead," she said. "The terrorist was right on top of him when it happened. There's no way he survived. In fact, he tried to intervene, and the terrorist ended up chasing him into the middle of the auditorium. If he'd pushed him backward, the bomb might have gone off in the hallway or even the lobby instead of here." She held the bandage to her cheek.

"That's enough for now, Allison," Seles said. "Let's go get you looked at." He led her away with a significant look at Bolan that basically said, "Now what?"

The first responders began to swarm around them, gathering up the last of the injured. Bolan worked his way through the rubble to what had been the center of the auditorium. The communications center was completely destroyed. Any data or evidence or even patterns they'd been running was gone. Any hope of working as a coordinated team to catch the terrorists was erased.

Bolan felt that this entire situation was outrageous. All they'd done was run from bad lead to bad lead, getting nowhere, getting distracted. He'd been playing too nice while the terrorists behind this were playing hardball. They'd started riots, blown up a train, given out false leads and even destroyed the EOC—all to keep law enforcement too busy to track them. These were terrorists, intent on killing Americans. Somewhere in all the chaos, that simple fact had been lost.

Bolan turned on his heel. It was time to stop playing their game and start playing his. Hart was right—they'd been going about this all wrong, playing it by the book. Even he'd been wrapped up in it. Striding to where Hart was being treated, he tapped Seles on the shoulder. "She's right," he said.

"About what?" Seles asked.

"We've been chasing them. It's time to turn it around. We have to draw them out."

"How do we do that?" he asked, looking askance at the rubble. "They've been one step ahead of us the whole time."

"Leave that to me," Bolan said. "I'll call you later. Where are you going to set up?"

"The police station," Hart said.

"Fine," he replied. "I'm stealing your vehicle, Denny. Keep your phone on. I'll need you soon." Feeling more himself than he had since this mess started, he turned and headed for Seles's SUV. It was time for the Executioner to play by his own rules—the rules of the predator and the hunter. The rules of a man who'd faced down every challenge he met and taken out every evil he'd encountered.

WITH SEATING FOR UP TO seventy thousand people for a football game, Ford Field was a beautiful stadium that had hosted Super Bowls, rock concerts, basketball games and even major soccer events. The design was unique in that it incorporated a previously existing warehouse into the construction, creating a space for high-end suites and lounges for those who could afford such luxuries. The owners were conscientious about security, and that stadium—in spite of it being symbolic of the capitalistic, crass nature of America—had become almost like a second home to Sayf. Of course, everyone here knew him as Michael Jonas.

This day was certain to draw a capacity crowd. The game had been sold out for months, and it was Halloween. He'd already ordered extra staff for the day, to ensure that the thousands of people in attendance could be carefully monitored and controlled. The main security office was a smaller version of the emergency operations center, though it lacked the auditorium style of design. Instead, two walls were covered with monitors that relayed camera information from different areas of the building: the parking lot, entrances and exits, concessions, the field itself and even the hallways in the luxury suites. The cameras were on automatic timers, panning back and forth on a predictable schedule, though from the control room, he could manually take over any individual camera and control it directly.

The game was scheduled to kick off at noon, Central Time, and the National Football League was very, very serious about things moving on time. Which was fine, as today of all days, time was quite important to him, as well. Sayf sat at one of the main stations and scrolled through the various screens. Fans were already gathering in the parking lot, preparing for the day's festivities in spite of the riots still popping up along 8 Mile Road and the train-yard fire, which was still burning in a few places. Americans, he'd learned, were as dedicated about their pleasures—perhaps more so—as they were about anything else. Nothing short of a massive disaster would keep them away on this day. As far as he was concerned, the more the merrier. And the more dead bodies that would be left behind in the rubble of the explosion.

The phone inside his suit coat began to vibrate. He carried a different phone on his hip that he used specifically for the Michael Jonas identity. This call would be for Sayf. For the moment, there was only one other security man in the office—and he was wearing a headset as he worked through the patrols for the day with another man, who was off inspecting the concessions area.

"Report," he said when he answered.

An excited Yasim responded. "Our mission is complete, Sayid. We have the detonators, and the EOC was destroyed just over an hour ago. We have everything we need now."

"No problems?" he asked.

"No, everything is in hand."

"Excellent. You have done well, my friend. Everything has been moved to the warehouse for final assembly?"

"Yes, everything is in position and the completion is taking place as we speak. We are on schedule."

Curious, Sayf asked, "What is the status of the personnel from the EOC?"

"It's on the news," he said. "There are more than thirty dead, though Allison Hart survived the blast and is still leading the response."

A wave of relief washed over him. His gamble had worked. It had been entirely possible that the suicide bomber would kill her, too, but it was a necessary risk to remove the NSA man who might have complicated matters. "Very good," he said. "I need you to start the next phase." He glanced over at the other man and saw that his headset was still on and he was firmly ensconced in his conversation.

"Take some of the men to 8 Mile Road. That area should be the main concern of the police. If you keep the fires and fights going, they will be forced to divert more of their resources to that area and their communication will be limited because of our successes. Remember, tonight is Devil's Night, so be sure to use those fears as a catalyst."

"Yes, Sayid. It will be done as you order," Yasim said, then he disconnected the call.

Sayf switched the monitors to the local news channels and watched his masterpiece coming together. There had never been a terrorist attack planned with such precision and care. The police, fire and ambulances raced around town and two of the emergency rooms had set up triage in their parking lots to deal with the victims from the EOC explosion as well as the steady flow of injured coming out of 8 Mile.

He smiled as the camera showed the ruins of the EOC building. His masterpiece was almost complete.

HAL BROGNOLA CHOMPED HEAVILY on his cigar as he watched the news broadcasts from Detroit. He punched up city maps and began connecting the dots of all of the attacks. The riots were obviously being managed—they popped up, went down, then reappeared in a different block of the same street over and over again. Things were spiraling out of control and so far, he hadn't heard from Bolan, who might very well have been caught in the blast at the EOC. His hotline rang and he groaned to himself before he answered.

"Mr. President," he said.

"Brognola, what the hell is going on? I thought your man was going to get this mess under control."

"Yes, sir. Last I heard from him, he was working on it, but getting arrested by the NSA kind of put a crimp in his investigation. His hot lead has gotten colder by the minute and now with the EOC shot to hell there is new information coming in, sir. I'm still waiting to get an update from the ground that's more than just raw data."

"I don't give a good goddamn what's shot to hell. Detroit is turning into Beirut and I want it stopped right *now*. Under Posse Comitatus, I can't send in troops, but I may not have a choice. The governor has already requested help from the National Guard."

"I'm not sure that's going to serve our best interests, sir," Brognola said. He explained his theory about how everything was being carefully managed by the terrorists. "It would almost be better if I could convince law enforcement to pull back and resume their normal patrols. The way it is now, a lot of the city is vulnerable because of how the police and emergency crews are positioned."

The President paused for a moment, then said, "I'll tell the governor to hold off, if that's your advice, Hal, but let's get this thing under control and find these bastards before Detroit turns into a war zone. That town has enough problems without adding mass disaster to it, as well."

"Thank you, Mr. President. As soon as I have an update, I'll call you."

"See to it, Brognola," he said, then hung up.

The big Fed turned his attention back to the news. "Come on, Striker," he said to himself. "Give me *something* to work with."

17

"Hang tight for a minute, Allison," Seles said, setting off after Bolan at a quick jog. They didn't have much time to waste, and Hart already had her cell phone in hand, working to set up a temporary EOC in an old dispatch station at the police department. While they assumed she was back in charge of coordination and Seles was in charge of field ops, they still needed official confirmation from the White House, which they'd been told was forthcoming.

Bolan had reached the back of Seles's SUV and opened it, checking over the equipment stores before heading out into the field. His face was a grim mask of determination, and the streaks of soot on his dark features looked more like war paint than evidence of a disaster. This was a man at home in the most deadly of circumstances, and despite his low-key approach so far, Seles sensed that he was a lot more than he appeared to be.

"This is a solid setup," Bolan said. "A little lean on weapons, but solid enough."

"We keep the anti-tank weapons at the office," Seles quipped. "But in all seriousness, do you think you can chase this whole thing down on your own? Give me a little time, Cooper, and we can do this together."

"I think we're out of options, Denny. No offense, but between the red tape of working by the book and the fact that everyone is stretched so thin, I don't think that your men could bring down a jaywalker right now. These guys have been two steps ahead of us for too long—it's time to run them to ground." He retrieved his Desert Eagle from where Seles had stored it earlier and checked the loads, returning it to the holster rig he was wearing.

"Fair enough," Seles said. "But field ops on this situation is still my command, and I need to try and keep some of it coordinated. Right now, I think our best bet is to get a handle on the riots. If we can do that, then I can free up some of my men, as well as law enforcement, for more active investigation of the terrorists. I still have guys at the main office running up the details for the weapons we should be looking for. If we can get the information on the actual explosive or the detonator then it may give us a place to start."

Bolan looked at the devastated building and shook his head. "My gut tells me that if we don't find these guys before noon, the riots are going to be the least of our concerns. This has been too well-executed. All of the moves on the chess board are right and now it's time for him to bring out the big guns while we're most vulnerable."

"Maybe, maybe not. But I can only throw resources at the problems I *know* about. Keep me updated and I'll get you as much support as I can."

"Will do," Bolan said. "But I need to be clear about this now. If any of your people get in my way I'll go straight through them. We're out of time. This—all of this—has been one long running feint. None of it matters to the terrorists except as a way to keep our eyes off them."

"I don't disagree with you, but until we can pin down a real lead, the best we can do is put out the fires we can see, figuratively and literally. If you get something solid, call me and I'll give you everything I can."

Bolan nodded. "Good luck," he said.

"You, too," Seles replied. "And stay safe out there. The streets are dangerous."

"So am I," Bolan replied, getting behind the wheel and gunning the engine as he headed out to track the man who had slipped through their fingers.

Seles turned and headed back toward Hart. The sun was climbing into the morning sky, though it felt to him like a cloudy day. A dark, cloudy day with a storm that just wouldn't end.

BOLAN KNEW THAT his first stop had to be back at the mosque to talk to Imam Al-Qadir. In spite of his spiritual conflict, the imam knew far more about this area and the people in it than he did. Bolan also suspected that if he was pushed, the imam knew far more about people like Batin than he wanted to admit. Nothing he'd seen had made him believe that the imam was a bad man; on the contrary, his community work was inclusive and open, and he'd tried to help Bolan, even when someone he knew was a potential target. His conflict stemmed from wanting to do the right thing for his mosque and his faith, not from a conflict about doing right in and of itself.

As he drove, he attached his handheld to the dash, and tapped the autodial for Brognola, who answered before the first ring had even finished.

"Striker, thank God," he said. "What's your status?"

"Not blown up with the EOC, thanks for asking," he said. "Allison and Denny are regrouping, and I'm back in the field."

"How bad was it?" Brognola asked.

"Pretty ugly," Bolan replied. "Over thirty dead, lots more injured. Basically, emergency management is out of the game for now. And we lost all of our data, including the models they were building."

"Do you have any leads?"

"I'm going to track down this Batin guy again, even if I have to tear the city apart to do it. What do you have for me?"

"I pulled everything we've got on Malick Yasim," he said. "This is a genuine bad man, Striker. He's been connected to killings and terrorist activities from L.A. all the way to Afghanistan. He's called the Mummy, because he looks like the guy from that movie. Only one thing."

"What's that?"

"He's not the leader—or probably isn't. He's strictly the second-in-command, muscle type. Chances are he's working for someone else."

"Great," Bolan said. "So another link in the chain, but not the end of it."

"Sorry, but I doubt it. One thing for sure is that he's the real deal. He's on every watch list in the world, but the CIA lost him late last year in Yemen. They had the idea of trying to turn him, but he wasn't receptive, and he killed their operative when he revealed himself. Anyway, watch your ass if you find him."

"I'll find him, Hal," Bolan said. "It's just a matter of time."

"Is it time we can afford?"

"I doubt it, but it's all we've got right now. I'll keep digging if you give me anything else."

Bolan thought about it. "This is too well-organized for Yasim to have only been here a few months," he said. "Is there any way you can think of that you can backtrack him from Yemen, maybe trace where he was before that?"

"I'll make some calls and see what I can find out," Brognola said.

"Good. I'll update you as soon as I have Batin," Bolan said, then hung up as he pulled into the parking lot behind Al-Qadir's mosque.

The back entrance door of the mosque hung by the remains of one hinge. Bolan pulled the Desert Eagle from his holster and did a quick survey of the parking area before moving inside. The beautiful tapestries of the mosque had been yanked from the walls or torn into pieces, and the hallway leading to the imam's office was spray-painted with the word *Traitor* in Arabic.

Bolan's heart sank as he moved down the corridor and saw a figure lying in the doorway of the imam's office. He rushed forward and knelt next to the battered imam.

As Bolan rolled him over gently, the man's breath came in shallow gasps. He'd been stabbed at least three times and the front of his shirt was covered in blood. His eyes were shut and his lips moved in soundless prayer.

"Al-Qadir," Bolan said. "It's me, Cooper."

The imam's eyes fluttered weakly and he slowly opened the one that wasn't swollen shut.

"Cooper…they know…and they…"

"Who did this?"

"Batin. They know about you. They are evil. They…desecrated a holy place. Allah will not protect them now." These last few words came out in a rush as he struggled to breathe.

"Where will they go? Can you help me find them?"

"There…is one place. A place they call holy, but it is…a den of hate. It's on 8 Mile Road. They go there to plot…hate."

"I need to find them fast. I need more, Al-Qadir," Bolan said, trying to will the dying man to live long enough to tell him.

The imam struggled to breathe and began to fade in and out of consciousness. Bolan flipped open his phone and dialed Seles as he tried to coax the imam back into the land of the living. The call went straight to voice mail. "Where is this place, my friend? I need you to tell me where."

The imam coughed and blood pooled at the corners of his mouth as his breathing came in hard, short rasps. Bolan propped the imam up farther to try to ease the pressure on his ruined lungs. The holy man stirred and coughed again. The blood was bright red and Bolan didn't think he had much time left. He could hear that one of his lungs had collapsed and the sucking sound every time the man took a breath was not bringing him the life-giving air that he needed.

"I need the location. I need to know where to find Batin."

"They call it…a sanctuary," he huffed. "Old abandoned mansion…Woodward Avenue. Stop them. No time left." The imam's words died away as his heart gave out. Bolan pulled him into the safety of his office. Pulling a beautiful tapestry off the wall, he used it as a shroud to cover the imam's body.

He stalked out of the office and pulled out his cell phone as he made his way to the SUV. Seles picked up the phone this time, but Bolan could barely hear him over the chaos in the background.

"What the hell is going on there?" Bolan shouted.

"Anarchy. The riots have practically turned into their own war zone, and with limited communication we're pulling our police back to defensive positions just trying to keep it from spreading farther. Our emergency rooms are flooded and we can't seem to put a cap on it."

"Well, I'm heading right into the thick of it. I have a lead on a hidden mosque. My guess is that whoever is behind all of this today is adding fuel to the fire. If we can cut off the head of the snake, the body will die."

"I can't send anyone in to help you. You'll be on your own, Cooper, until I can get there."

"You should stay out of it," Bolan said. "Pull all your men back and let the residents settle it for themselves. They'll help you when they see that they have no choice and that they aren't the ones starting it."

"I can't do that, Cooper," he said. "Call me if you get something solid."

Bolan rounded the corner on Dearborn and wished his

vehicle of choice had been an armored Humvee instead of a bulletproof SUV. The street was littered with broken glass, two cars were on fire, and as his dark SUV rolled down the street, rioters threw bottles and rocks at it and even a hub cap screeched along the glass of his windshield, leaving a scar. Bolan punched the accelerator and smashed through the debris blocking the road. Pedestrians cleared the way and Bolan heard a bullet bounce off his armored doors.

The chaos thinned as he approached the mosque. Turning off his headlights, he eased closer to the building. The streetlights were out and the fires from the cars and debris no longer cast long shadows to help guide his path. Bolan scanned the old mansion. Typical for a turn-of-the-century building, the roof had a sag, but the columns still held true, giving the old house some structural integrity.

Men were entering the mosque in their prayer vestments, but no cars were parked in the front. He needed a closer look, but couldn't risk his quarry going to ground again. He needed to get ahead of the wave of disaster before the whole city was rolled up in it.

18

The office of Michael Jonas boasted plush carpet on the floor, a beautiful desk of cherrywood, comfortable chairs, a bank of monitors that allowed him access to direct feeds from the main security booth as well as television, and even a small wet bar for when the day had been long enough to warrant the reward of a drink. Michael Jonas had been known to have a Scotch at the end of a long day, though Sayid Rais Sayf was a teetotaler. At the moment, he was alone, listening to updates from his security officers via the handheld radio sitting on his desk. So far, the morning had been relatively quiet, with only a handful of the fans in the parking lot requiring even a warning to tone it down to a more sedate party.

None of that changed the nervous energy that was pulsing through his body as he paced the floor like a caged tiger. Even as the final preparations were made to complete his mission, he worried that some vital step may have been overlooked. The anticipation building inside him competed with his fears that he might somehow fail. Still, even with minor mistakes along the way, he could not have asked for his plans to succeed any better than they had. Kickoff for the football game was just a bit more than three hours away, and shortly after that, a holy, cleansing fire. Allah would be pleased with his work.

On one of the monitors, a local news channel was covering the fire at the train yard. The fire department was reporting that it was now ninety percent contained, and there was no further danger to the closest neighborhoods. He added that fire crews would likely be on the scene for the next ten to twelve hours with the last of the containment and cleanup. The news camera panned over the devastation, and in the background, firemen wearing heavy protective gear could be seen working with special hoses to deal with the chemical spill. So far, so good, Sayf thought.

He used the phone on his desk to dial Hart's cell. When she answered, her voice was clipped and tired.

"Allison! My God, are you all right?" he exclaimed. "I've been trying to reach you ever since I heard."

"I'm fine, Michael, just some bumps and bruises—and a handful of stitches. I wish I had time to talk with you, but this is a big mess, as you can imagine."

"I'm sure," he said. "I've been horribly worried. Is there anything I can do? What all is happening? The city seems to be coming apart, though you wouldn't know it from the fans here!" Privately, Sayf cringed at the tone in his voice. He despised playing the role of doting boyfriend.

"I can't really talk much about it right now," she said. "We're putting together a temporary EOC at the moment."

"I understand, of course. You know I only want to help and sometimes having a sounding board is a good way to make certain you haven't missed something. With all of this chaos it's easy to miss things."

Sayf's gentle coaxing paid off as Hart moved to a quieter area and began spilling her guts. "Right now," she admitted, "everything's a mess. There are riots up and down 8 Mile Road, the EOC is destroyed all of our emergency crews and law-enforcement personnel are exhausted and stretched to their limits. Our only hope right now is that our one lead pans out in time to do something about it."

"You have a lead?" he asked, trying to keep his voice calm.

"A small one. We think this man named Batin has more information, if Cooper, the agent hunting for him, can get to him in time."

"So you know where he is?"

"We think so. An imam who runs a mosque on 8 Mile revealed the location of a hidden prayer center just before he died—killed by the same people that are responsible for all of this. I just hope at this point the information was worth his sacrifice."

Trying not to feel panicked, Sayf said, "Oh yes, I hope so, too."

"I don't know, Michael," Allison said. "I think this has all been too much. The governor is making noises about bringing in the National Guard to help lock down the whole city until all of this calms down. Perhaps..." Her voice trailed off in thought.

"Perhaps?" he nudged when the silence began to stretch out.

"Perhaps we *should* cancel the game today. That's an awful lot of people gathered in one place. I'd be happy to call the owners and talk with them to explain the situation."

"I've given that a lot of thought, too, Allison, but it would be quite difficult at this point. We're at full capacity today and the parking lot is already full of tailgaters. I think the best way to steady everyone's nerves is to keep things as normal as possible. I rather doubt that the public has connected all of these events, and cancelling the game might cause a panic or problems here that even my team couldn't handle."

She considered his words for a few seconds, then said, "You're right, of course. Maybe the distraction of the game will help keep people calm. The people of Detroit love football, and cancelling the game would require explanations to a lot of people."

"Indeed," he agreed. "I don't want to keep you from your duties. Perhaps you'll find time to call later on today?"

"I'll try," she said. "Stay safe, Michael, and let me know immediately if there are any problems there."

"I will," he said, hanging up the phone. His frown could have frozen water as he removed the cell phone in his jacket and dialed Batin's number. It was time that they took care of this Matt Cooper, the man who had been on their trail all night…once and for all.

FROM HIS VANTAGE POINT, Bolan watched as the last few men entered the mansion. With the sun now fully in the sky, getting in unseen could prove very difficult. He started the SUV and drove around the block, wanting to take a look at the back of the building. Fortunately, he saw that there was an alley between the mansion and the next lot over, which was occupied by another old mansion, though this one appeared long-abandoned. Many of the houses in this neighborhood had once been nice, but now were either empty foreclosures or tenements barely suitable for living. He parked the SUV near a row of trees and got out, stopping at the back long enough to grab a Taser X26. If Batin tried to run, he wanted to make certain to bring him down alive.

Slipping through the trees and through the neighboring lot, Bolan saw that the alley between the houses was crowded with trash as well as several vehicles. There was plenty of cover to choose from and the sun hadn't crested high enough to fill the shadows in the alley. He paused to watch the building again for several minutes, looking for sentries. When he didn't see any, he moved into the alley, closing in on the mansion where Batin was hiding. Through the thin walls, he could hear the muffled sound of an Islamic prayer service.

Bolan's eyes scanned the house for an entry point. He spotted a long-disused ladder running up the back and onto the roof. Sometimes the Fates worked *in* his favor, and he'd learned to accept those blessings whenever they happened. Far too often, the opposite was true. He slipped out of the alley and was up the ladder in seconds, pausing only once when it gave a rather alarming creak. Inside, the voices droned on, so far unaware of his presence.

The roof itself was in horrible shape, but he quickly found what he was looking for: a set of skylights that looked down into the house itself. He moved silently, placing each step with care, as there were any number of places where the roof looked weak and one where the shingles and subroof were gone, allowing him to see down into an empty kitchen. Once he reached the skylights, he peered through each one until he spotted Batin.

The man's hand was wrapped in a fiberglass cast, and rather than participating in the worship service, he was standing in the far back of the room, watching the proceedings with a vaguely disinterested gaze. The imam who was giving the service said, *"Nauzubillah"*—Allah protect us—and Batin mouthed the word in response. Bolan thought that when he was done with him, Allah might be the only help left for the man.

There were at least twenty men in the room below, so a full-on assault was out of the question. First, it was entirely possible that some, perhaps most of them, were simply here to worship in whatever way they felt comfortable and had no idea what Batin and Yasim and whoever else was involved were doing. Second, he wanted to capture Batin as quietly as possible. Considering that the terrorists always seemed to be one step ahead, a shadow op would be the best approach.

Bolan continued watching as he contemplated his options. Suddenly, Batin jerked in surprise, then pulled a cell phone out of his jacket. The ring or vibration had caught him off guard and he was likely already feeling paranoid. He held the phone to his ear and listened for a minute, saying something that Bolan couldn't hear. Then his eyes widened, and he began shouting instructions.

Men ran in all directions, and weapons began appearing from nowhere. Batin had been warned about something or someone and was currently on full alert. "Damn it," Bolan muttered under his breath. "How's he getting his information?"

It didn't matter at the moment. Bolan needed to stay hidden and keep his eyes on his target. From the far side of the roof, he heard the sound of someone coming up the ladder. He moved to the back side of a chimney where he could keep an eye through the skylight on Batin. A tall, lean man climbed onto the roof, and Bolan wondered if his luck was going to hold and the man would simply take a look and go back down, but as the man started walking toward his hiding place, he saw that the Fates had once more decreed that the hard way was a lot more common than the easy one.

He slipped his combat knife out of his boot, tucking it back along his arm, and waited, holding himself perfectly still. Bolan's dark clothing and the chimney provided a good, shadowed cover. The man walking toward him was peering about the yard more than the roof, trying to see down into the alley and the streets around the property itself. Bolan waited until he was close, then stepped in behind him.

The shingles on the roof split beneath his boots at the sudden movement, and the grating sound was loud enough to give the man a second of warning. He spun and stutter-stepped backward, causing Bolan's knife strike to miss by a half inch. Knowing that any sound of alarm would compromise his position, Bolan leapt forward, trying to silence the man before he could make any noise.

The man's arms pinwheeled wildly as he tried to catch his balance and fend the Executioner off at the same time. Stepping closer, Bolan brought the knife in low, and the blade sliced through the man's sweater, shirt and the flesh below to his target—the diaphragm muscle. The man's breath left him in a rush, his scream of warning cut off before he could sound the alarm.

Pulling the blade back, Bolan was moving in to catch hold of him when the man's feet went out from beneath him completely, the roof shingles giving way, and he fell over backward—and through the ancient skylight. The crash of broken glass and the thud of his body were followed by a brief, stunned silence from those below, followed by at least two dozen angry shouts of outrage.

Bolan looked down and saw Batin meet his gaze. They stared at each other for a long two or three seconds, then the spell broke. Batin shouted, pointing at the roof, and made a run for the door.

As the angry men boiled out of the house, Bolan ran for the ladder, knowing that if Batin escaped this time, it might well be impossible to catch him again.

SELES'S SUV SKIDDED TO A HALT as he tried to make another corner on his way to help Bolan, only to find the street blocked with overturned cars and small fires in the surrounding debris. One fire truck had already been attacked and the crew forced to evacuate and leave the truck in the hands of the gang members.

Seles picked up his phone and called Hart.

"Allison, what we're doing isn't working. I think Cooper's right. We have to pull everyone back."

"What are you talking about?" she asked, stunned. "If we pull back, we'll leave the residents defenseless."

"But the residents aren't doing this!" he explained. "They're hunkered down in their houses. These are roving gangs that disappear before we can get to them. If we pull back and set up a perimeter, the residents will help because it's *their* neighborhood. They might be poor, but most of them are just normal folk and right now they're staying in and they're scared."

She hesitated, then said, "You're in charge of field ops, Denny, but I want it on record that I'm not fully in favor of this."

"It's the only way to keep our crews safe, Allison. It will give us a chance to regroup. Right now, everyone is spread out and separated, running from one problem to another."

"We can't just leave all the civilians in there to suffer. We have to get fire and EMS to them."

"Allison, you're not hearing me. If we don't do something soon there will be no fire or EMS left. Now set up a perimeter with the reserves and call me back with the details. If we pull back, the locals will see that they are going to need to put their differences aside to get all of this handled."

"All right. I'll do it, but I don't like it."

"I didn't say that you had to like it, just do it and then get back to me." He hung up the phone and put the SUV in Reverse. One way or another, he was going to get to Bolan.

19

Batin was out the back door and heading for the alley by the time Bolan was halfway down the ladder. Below, a good two dozen understandably angry Islamic men were shouting curses. He knew that if he was to have any hope of catching his prey, he'd have to back them off quickly before their anger turned to action and he found himself on the wrong end of a religiously inspired lynching. He slid down past the last few rungs, spinning and drawing his Desert Eagle as he landed.

It was a fairly large weapon, and the heavy, .40 caliber rounds made an impressively intimidating noise as he squeezed off two shots into the air. The crowd of men went silent as he covered them with the weapon. "Batin's a bad man and I'm a cop. Back off," he said, gesturing with the weapon to make his point.

The crowd of men murmured and began to back away, several of them using their cell phones. "Out of the way," Bolan growled, moving toward the alley. As soon as he was past them, he took off running, catching a bare glimpse of Batin as he cut right at the far end of the alley and through the trees.

Bolan broke into a sprint. He reached the point where Batin had cut in and spun, only to find himself confronted by the man, who'd apparently decided to stand and fight.

He'd picked up a heavy brick and threw it at Bolan's head. Bolan dodged, and the concrete block clipped the top of his right shoulder instead. A flare of pain burned in his arm, but Bolan kept moving, trying to get past the trees and into a more open area, even as he holstered the Desert Eagle.

Noise from behind warned Bolan that he had extra company. He dove forward, rolling, and came out on the other side of the trees. Batin lurched forward, having picked up another chunk of concrete, and two more men burst through the trees. Neither was armed, but both clearly had violence on their minds.

"Malick wants him dead!" Batin said, pointing at Bolan. "He's going to ruin everything we've worked for!"

Bolan kept moving, circling left, and drew his combat blade once more. The three men began to surround him, and that's when he made his move. Drawing the Taser X26 with his left hand, he didn't even bother with a verbal warning. He fired and the electrodes shot forward, taking Batin in the chest. The probes pierced his clothing and delivered the jolt that law enforcement called neuromuscular incapacitation— in short, Batin collapsed in a twitching heap, wetting himself in the process. He made an inarticulate grunting sound as he tried to scream.

As soon as Batin was down, Bolan dropped the Taser and turned his attention to the other two men, who were rapidly closing in on either side. Sidestepping, Bolan twisted, turned and took the legs out from beneath the man to his right in a simple leg sweep.

The second man grappled him, and Bolan turned into the hold, bringing the blade in low. He cut a swift arc, and the denim of the man's jeans parted like soft butter as the tender flesh of his inner thigh beneath them was cut. Blood began pouring immediately as he cursed and released Bolan. When he looked down and saw the damage, the man slapped his hands down on his thigh, a high whining sound in his voice, as he gibbered in fear. The artery had been cut and his life's blood was pouring out of his leg.

Bolan turned his attention back to the first man, who was getting to his feet. He judged the angle carefully, then delivered a short, vicious snap kick to the temple. The man collapsed, knocked out cold. He turned back to the bleeding man. "You'd best take off your belt and tourniquet that leg, or you'll be dead in a minute or two."

"Help me," he begged.

"Help yourself," Bolan replied. "I'm busy." He moved over to where Batin was still writhing on the ground, and knelt next to him, disengaging the Taser lines. "Hello, Batin," he said. "We never got to finish our talk."

The man didn't seem all that interested in answering at the moment, but Bolan knew that in due time, he'd be singing like the proverbial canary.

"I'LL GET HIM HERE!" Batin screeched as Bolan continued to question him.

Seles peered around the nearly empty warehouse. It would make a perfect trap if Batin could deliver Yasim as he promised. His only hope was that this wasn't yet another dead end, or worse still, a trap for them instead of a trap for the terrorists. A catwalk ran along the upper floor where the currently empty offices were located, though there was a temporary office of some kind set up in the middle, complete with a battle-scarred desk, two sides of cubicle walls, and a task chair that had seen better days about ten users or so ago. The crates or boxes that would normally fill the aisles were absent, which left little room for cover, but also few places for their prey to hide.

Bolan stepped away from where Batin was sitting on the floor. "I think we can make this work, Denny," he said.

"Is what he's told you about this Malick consistent with your other intelligence?" Seles asked.

"Batin's information matches what we know," Bolan said, referring to his handheld and looking over his notes. "According to what I've got, this Malick has been in the game for a number of years as a muscle for hire. Until a couple of years ago, he was doing whatever was asked of him for the highest bidder in places like Syria and Yemen. Then he sort of faded in and out of view and was using a variety of names to conduct his business. One thing is certain—he's a get-it-done kind of guy, and he loves a good jihad."

"Detroit doesn't seem like the kind of place he'd end up," Seles said.

Bolan nodded in agreement. "It's odd, but if whoever he's working for is playing a big enough game—and it appears that's the case—then he might have been attracted simply for the destruction potential."

"And Batin believes that Malick will respond to him?"

"Yes, he does. He's been running little errands for Malick for at least six months. He doesn't know who's pulling Malick's strings, but he does know that they've been planning something big for a long time." Bolan slipped the handheld back into his coat.

"Does he know any of the specifics?" Seles asked.

Bolan shook his head. "Not much. He did tell me that one of the jobs he did for Malick was acquiring various types of metal sheets, including aluminum, lead and titanium—all of which might be used in constructing a bomb, depending on the configuration of the device."

"Charming," Seles said. "Did he happen to actually *see* this bomb, or even hear Malick Yasim mention it?"

"Hardly," Bolan said. "But he knows that Malick mentioned today's date on several occasions as the big day for their cause. He put the rest together himself, which is one of the reasons he was trying to get out of town."

Seles nodded. "Well, I don't see that we have much to lose but time and dignity, and this is our only lead. Make the call with Batin, and let's see if we can get a rat to stick his head in our trap."

"Have your guys set up in hidden locations and maintain a perimeter once he's inside."

"It'll be a one-way street within five minutes," Seles promised.

"Good. Just remind them that we need this Malick alive. He's our last hope for finding the bomb."

"We'll get him, Cooper," he said. "You just see to it that Batin gets him here."

"I'll make sure of it," the Executioner said, turning back to Batin whose face went pale as Bolan approached.

FORD FIELD WAS FILLING UP FAST and the crowd was getting louder by the second. Far above where they were placing the bomb, the luxury suites were being populated with the rich, spoiled Americans who—in spite of all the terrors visited upon the city over the last day—felt secure in their safety and well-being. Sayf had expected as much, but Yasim had believed that many people would stay away from the stadium. Sayf's plan had apparently accounted for the arrogance of the Americans.

Yasim and four other men used a come-along attached to an electric winch driver to move the bomb into place. They used the crowd noise to cover their work as they mounted the bomb and the metal frame containing it to a support beam next to the junction of both power and gas lines under the stadium. This placement would create maximum impact, and the intense heat could potentially cause gas-line explosions and EMP power bursts throughout the connected network.

In other words, even if the bomb itself didn't kill you, the effects outside the immediate blast zone might.

Not that it mattered, Yasim thought as he worked. Thousands, perhaps hundreds of thousands, would die. It would make 9/11 look like the work of an angry child, and they would be remembered forever. In a very short time, their triumph would be complete, and he himself would be cradled in the warm bosom of Allah with his promised rewards.

His phone rang and Yasim saw that Batin was calling. He was expecting the good news that the DEA agent had been killed and everything was on schedule.

"Yes," he answered.

"Malick!" Batin cried. "Everything has gone wrong and I need you to get me out of here!"

'What do you mean?" he demanded. "What has gone wrong?"

"When I was warned that Cooper was still coming after me, I told all the men at the mosque that the government was spying on the building. They searched for him and one of your men went to the roof where Cooper killed him. Then he chased me down an alley where we fought. I barely managed to escape with my life!"

"What happened to the two others I assigned to protect the mosque?" Yasim said.

"He killed them cold," Batin said. "He just doesn't quit, Malick! Please, I need an extraction immediately."

Annoyed at the dismaying news, Yasim asked, "Where are you now?"

"The warehouse rendezvous point where I delivered the titanium sheets last month. Please Malick, I want to see this through to the end."

"Don't whine at me, Batin," he snapped. "Stay there and I will come and find you, but if they get to you first you know what you must do. He must be stopped. You must kill him or die in the attempt."

"I think I've lost him for now," he said. "But no matter where I go, he seems to find me. Just hurry, Malick."

Doing his best to keep the disgust from showing on his face, Yasim hung up the phone and faced Sayf, who was busily scrolling through the various status reports on his phone.

"What is it?" he asked, absently. "Did Batin kill Cooper?"

"No, sir. Apparently this man is more than he appears."

"I thought the FBI was being run by Denny Seles. Who is this man if he's not working for him?"

"We believe he is DEA," Yasim suggested. "Either way, I will go to Batin's location and end this. I will kill Cooper myself, then return here immediately."

"Where is Batin now?"

"In the warehouse on Twenty-Third."

"Do you believe he is alone? Could he be playing a double game?"

Yasim considered this, then nodded slowly. "It's possible, though Batin has seemed dedicated to our work. I will go and get him and neutralize Cooper."

"Very well, Malick, but I want Cooper dead and you back in one hour. If Batin is losing it, or your feel like he is playing with us, kill him on sight and hurry back here."

"I cannot believe Batin would betray us. You'll see. I will bring him back and we can work together until the end. We will join Allah together."

"I certainly hope so," Sayf said. "Why else go to all the trouble if not for His glory?"

20

Sayf finished supervising the installation of the bomb after Yasim left, then, with less than an hour until kickoff, returned to his duties as Security Director. Smuggling the bomb inside had been simple enough using equipment from the security and maintenance departments, along with the liberal use of tarps. No one had even looked twice at the men loading a large, heavy-duty cart at the private loading docks, and even fewer had looked once they were moving within the stadium itself. By keeping his radio on his person, he ensured constant contact with the regular security staff, who simply assumed he was doing rounds.

With everything in place Sayf stopped by the central security station to check in. In spite of the packed stadium and the sound of the chanting fans reverberating through the building, there were no significant troubles. Sayf had already instructed everyone that considering the situation in the city itself, they should strive to handle situations in a calm manner and do their best not to have to call the police. Everyone on his staff had agreed that was an excellent idea and Sayf couldn't help but smile at their blissful ignorance. On a normal Sunday, the police would be called—and at least two or three patrol units would be on site—to take away drunk and disorderly fans a half dozen or more times.

He returned to his office and offered his final pregame

assessment to the owners that all was well, then he sat down and took a deep breath. There was nothing more divine than this moment. Sayf logged into a subroutine on his computer and was able to view the camera he'd installed that focused directly on the bomb. From here, he could make sure that it was undisturbed until it was time to activate the detonator, which he would do in person.

On the ground in front of the bomb was a set of prayer rugs. The detonator was already set to do a five-minute countdown, and the device to activate it was a program built into his smartphone that used wireless signals. When it was time, he, Yasim and the rest of the men would go into the basement and pray together as the last moments of their time in this world trickled away. They would share their victory, just as they had shared the struggles of reaching this point.

Early on, he had considered detonating the weapon from a safe distance, but he wanted to be present, in the event that something went wrong. So many others in similar movements had failed because they lacked the courage to be a part of the sacrifice at the last minute. He and his men had trained for this for long months and years; none of them would be so cowardly.

Glancing at his watch, he picked up the phone and dialed Hart's number. She'd been unintentionally indispensible to his planning, but it would be wise to do one final check-in with her. Surprises were for the uninformed and the unprepared, Sayf believed, which is why dating her and slowly grilling her for information on how the emergency services for the city were coordinated had been crucial. He couldn't afford any last-second surprises, and this would be his last contact with her. Assuming she survived the blast—and there was absolutely no guarantee of that—he knew she would be implicated in the investigation that was sure to follow.

The video message he'd prepared for this day was clear

on her involvement. He wanted the world to know how he'd broken the system. The video would be automatically broadcast by a sympathetic friend in New York after the explosion occurred. The man didn't know what was going to happen, only that he was to watch the video when he saw the sign from Detroit that Islam had finally struck a telling blow against the hated Shayton, America.

She answered after several rings, sounding almost giddy. "Oh, Michael! I'm so glad you called!"

"Hello, Allison. You sound almost happy," he said, trying to keep the fear and suspicion out of his voice. "Something must have happened."

"It did!" she said, unable to contain the excitement in her voice. "I know I shouldn't tell you, I haven't even told the staff here yet, but we got Batin."

A surge of fear washed over him. If Batin was in custody… "Really, you must be thrilled. Are you bringing him back there for questioning?"

"Not yet," she said, gleefully. "The FBI has set a trap for one of the major players in this mess and they're about to spring it. I can't wait until all of these guys are in custody. This one calls himself the Mummy, can you believe it?"

Sweat broke out on Sayf's brow, but he had cautioned himself since the beginning against panic. If Yasim was taken into custody, that would be unfortunate, but not the end of everything. Still, he would prefer to have his second with him at the end. "I'm sure a name like that will make for even better stories after all of this is done," he said. "I'm sorry, Allison, but I just got paged for a security matter. I have to go, but I'll call you later."

He slammed down the phone, then quickly used his cell to dial Yasim. The initial call went to voice mail, and stunned at this rapid turn of events, he hung up and frantically dialed once again. One ring, two rings, then Yasim finally answered.

"Yes, Sayid?" he said, whispering.

He must be close to or inside the warehouse. "Malick, my brother, it's a trap!"

"What?"

"Batin has set you up. Kill him. Kill them all and then get back here immediately. We won't wait for halftime. We must act now!"

"It will be as you say," Yasim replied, then hung up.

Conflicts warred within him. If Yasim failed, the police or federal law enforcement could be there at any time, ready to do everything in their power to stop him. Still, the Mummy had never seriously failed him before. He looked at his watch and reminded himself once again that panic was the undoing of many plans.

He would wait, for a while at least, before he moved forward without Yasim. Nothing, even the loss of a trusted lieutenant, could be allowed to stop the bomb from going off.

FROM HIS POSITION inside the warehouse, Bolan watched as a midsize SUV pulled inside and slowed to a stop. Batin got up from the chair he'd been sitting on and started walking toward the vehicle. He was wired for sound, so he could hear Bolan's instructions. "Take it slow, Batin," he whispered. "Give him time to get out."

On the other side of the warehouse, up on the catwalk, Seles was in position with a Remington 700 tactical rifle with a low light scope, while outside, the rest of his team would be moving in on the warehouse perimeter to ensure that no one escaped. "Stay right with him, Denny," Bolan instructed.

A tall, bald man who could only be Malick Yasim got out of the SUV, then paused to take a call on his cell phone as Batin got closer to his friend, his arms open in greeting. Two more men also got out and the three of them started toward the center of the warehouse. Bolan saw something that caught his attention—a tiny hitch in Yasim's stride, a miniscule head tilt—but whatever it was, he knew the game was up as the Mummy turned his gaze toward the catwalk, while putting his cell phone away.

"Batin, he *knows*," Bolan hissed into his comm unit. "You need to try and get out of there slowly. Greet him and then tell him that you forgot something on the desk and turn around. If he so much as flinches I want you to drop to the ground and then find some cover." He watched as Batin's smile faded and he stumble-stepped. The whole situation was going to go bad in a hurry.

Bolan switched his comm-link channel to law-enforcement-only. "Seles, we've been made. Keep this guy in your sights." Batin and Yasim were now less than ten feet apart.

"From this angle, I don't have anything but a kill shot," he whispered.

Bolan let out a held breath. "Then hold unless there's no other choice. We need this guy alive."

"Understood."

Bolan watched as Batin greeted Yasim with a kiss on either cheek. "I'm so grateful you came to me, my friend," he said.

"Allah will always protect those that are loyal to him."

"Allahu Akbar!" Batin said. "Of course."

"It is unfortunate that you were not loyal," he said. "You are damned."

Batin didn't have a chance. Bolan never saw where the knife came from, probably Yasim's sleeve, but he struck with the speed and precision of a trained killer. He clasped Batin by the back of the head, and drove it up and inward, directly between the third and fourth rib. If his lung wasn't punctured or his heart pierced, Batin would have screamed in agony. As it was, he slumped into the Mummy's arms, blood leaking from his mouth.

Bolan was already in motion as he called, "Damn it! Denny, take a shot!"

The .308 rifle fired once, the report echoing through the warehouse, and taking out one of Yasim's henchman in a spray of blood and bone that looked like a red cloud. The second henchman pulled a gun and ran toward the catwalk, firing wildly and screaming about Allah.

Yasim spun, throwing Batin's limp body at Bolan as a shield, and drawing his own gun from a lower back holster. Bolan dove to his right, dodging past Batin, and came up close enough to knock the gun out of Yasim's grasp with a fast chop to his wrist. It fired once, high and wide, then spun away.

"Die!" he snarled, grappling with the Executioner.

Bolan drove a hard left into his midsection, a blow that would have taken the breath out of most men, but Yasim was a trained killer and his abs absorbed the blow as easily as a professional boxer. Hands closed around Bolan's throat and he slipped his arms up between them, pushing his enemy's arms wide, then followed up with a knife hand to the base of his neck.

Yasim stumbled backward two steps, and Bolan pressed his advantage, wanting to end it quickly, but his opponent recovered, coming up with a thin fighting blade in each hand. Bolan drew his own combat knife and circled, while Yasim's blades flickered and flashed in a style that looked like an odd combination of Spetsnaz and Jendo, but was uniquely his own. It mattered little to Bolan, who operated under the philosophy that a knife fight was far more dangerous than even a gun—and a well-trained knife fighter was deadly.

"I will send you to hell," Yasim said between his clenched teeth.

Bolan said nothing, waiting and ready for the man's next move.

Screaming, the Mummy closed and the Executioner backed

a bit and slid sideways, using his own larger knife to deflect two strikes. His follow-up missed, however, and Yasim scored a cut on the back of Bolan's arm before dancing away.

In his earpiece, Seles said, "The other guy's down. Do you want me to take the shot?"

"No," he said, his eyes never leaving the man who was intent on killing him. Needing Yasim alive complicated the fight immensely and the longer it went on, the more dangerous it would become for Bolan. He watched for an opening as they clashed several more times and he realized that Yasim's reputation was well-deserved. He was an expert with his blades, and several times it was only through speed and skill of his own that Bolan managed to avoid a serious injury.

By this point, Yasim had to know that he was trapped and he seemed determined to go down fighting.

"Give it up, Malick," Bolan said. "I can do this all day, or have one of the feds shoot you."

"Then tell them to shoot," Yasim said, smiling. "I will die and you will learn nothing."

Bolan started to say something more, trying to distract the killer, when he accidentally stumbled over Batin's body. The one mistake was more than enough of an opening for Yasim.

Tripping, Bolan fell over and tried to continue the movement, but the man known as the Mummy was on top of him in a flash. Without his own knife, which he'd had to drop, Bolan had no choice but to grasp Yasim's wrists. Both men were strong, but leverage and position gave the advantage to the terrorist and his blades inched closer and closer to Bolan's exposed throat.

"I have a shot," Seles said in his ear.

"No!" Bolan shouted, trying to force the blades back. In the dim light of the warehouse, he could see the razor-sharp edges gleaming.

"I have a shot," Seles repeated.

"Don't," the Executioner said, straining with his whole body, but Yasim wasn't giving an inch.

The blades pushed down, flashing one last time as Yasim twisted his wrists and escaped Bolan's grasp. They rushed down, twin messengers of death.

It's over, Bolan thought wildly. *One stupid mistake.* Then the shot from Seles's rifle cut the air and the back of Yasim's head exploded.

His body slumped over to one side and Bolan pushed him the rest of the way off, glad to be alive, but stunned at the end result.

Their last lead was dead. And somewhere in Detroit, a nuclear bomb was about to go off.

21

Seles came down from the catwalk with the rifle slung over one shoulder. "I didn't have a choice, Cooper," he said as Bolan got to his feet. "He was going to cut your throat and the head shot was the best angle."

Bolan removed his shirt and wiped the blood spatter off his face, shaking his head. "I know," he said. "But now we're in serious trouble. The chain doesn't end with Malick and we don't have a clue as to where the bomb is."

Crossing the floor, he picked up the knife he'd dropped and slid it back into the sheath on his boot. With Batin and Yasim dead, they were stuck. This operation should have been simple and flawless, but nothing in this mission had gone that way. Murphy's Law was one thing, and sometimes things just didn't work out, but that's not what this was. This was a case of everyone being caught flat-footed by a terrorist operation and no one having enough information to cut the bad guys off at the knees.

"It would've been nice to leave at least one of them alive," he muttered, as much to himself as Seles.

"You're complaining about the body count?" Seles said. "You're welcome, by the way."

Bolan paced back and forth. "Sorry," he said. "And thank you. I'm just trying to get a handle on how this entire situation could have gone wrong from the beginning."

"We just haven't had enough information," Seles said.

"No, it's more than that. My gut says someone else is involved."

"Are you just being paranoid?"

"No," Bolan replied. "No, I don't think so. I had the same feeling back at the mosque. Think about it, every time we've started to close in, these guys would rabbit. They've been reacting to information that they shouldn't have had. When I took Batin into custody…if they'd known I was on the roof, they would have tried to neutralize me directly. Instead, they were just running from shadows."

"Maybe," Seles replied, sounding unconvinced. "But no one even knew about what we were doing here, so there was no information to react to."

Both men paused as they considered this, and realized in the same moment who'd been feeding the information to the terrorists.

"Allison Hart," Bolan said. "It has to be."

Seles tried to defend her, in spite of how it looked. "Come on, Cooper. I've known her for almost five years! She's not playing for the other team. She couldn't be. It's not in her character."

"It's the only thing that makes sense, Denny," he said. "We've kept her informed of everything happening in the field all day long. Just like we're supposed to do when we're all on the same team."

"Yeah, but…"

"But nothing," Bolan said. "She's the only person outside of your team here and myself who knew we were going to use Batin to trap Malick. She talked to someone."

Denial warred with acceptance on Seles's face for a moment, then acceptance won. "You're right," he said. "I don't like it and can hardly believe it, but… This whole time! She's been feeding them information this whole time. Do you know how many good people we've lost today?"

"Too many," the Executioner said. "But we're going to lose a lot more if we don't put a stop to all of this. Have your guys clean up here and we'll head back to the station to deal with Allison."

"Should I call and have her taken into custody?" Seles asked.

"Absolutely not!" Bolan said. "We don't know who else could be involved, and we definitely want her in our hands before she can find a way to alert her friends."

"I'm just sorry that it's come to this, Cooper. You've been running in circles all day, trying to keep us in the loop, and then we find out that she's working for the other side."

"The day isn't over yet," Bolan replied. "Let's go end this and all the running will be worth it."

THE COMMUNICATIONS ROOM at the police station was overrun with personnel trying to make certain that their station for the emergency operation center was getting the attention that it needed. Bolan didn't wait his turn in line to see Hart, but went straight to the front and grabbed her arm. The Executioner held on to his cool as he marched her down the hall with her staff watching. There was no time for delicacy.

Seles had already arranged an interrogation room and Bolan pulled her down the hallway and into the room and pushed her into a chair. Seles shut the door behind them and nodded at Bolan, indicating that the audio for the room had been cut, as well. They wanted to keep the situation as contained as possible.

"What the hell is the matter with you?" Hart shouted. "I'm in the middle of trying to run an operation."

"Yeah, we know," Bolan said. "It's just that your operation and ours aren't the same, are they?"

"What are you talking about?"

"We want to know about the other operation," Seles said.

"Denny, have you gone crazy?" she asked.

"You know, the one that's designed to take down the whole city with your help."

Hart stood up and put her hands on her hips. "Okay, boys, I don't know what you're thinking, but why doesn't someone come out and say it so we can quit playing games? Don't we have enough problems already? I've got a city up in flames, staff in the hospital and a building that is supposed to be the nerve center for coordinating all of this left in ruins."

Bolan carefully watched her every move. Her frustration was obviously rising, but there were no indications of fear or guilt. She was either a true believer or they were wrong. He didn't have time to be wrong and needed to know about her part in it and fast.

"Allison, we've been friends for quite a while, so it kills me to say this, but we know that you're feeding information to the terrorists. I have ops running traces on your cell phone right now so you might as well tell us everything," Seles said.

"I'm not…" she stammered.

"Listen to me carefully, Allison," Bolan said. "You already know we're out of time and out of leads, and frankly, I ran out of patience about six hours ago. I have no qualms about finding a way to make you talk."

"That…you…" she said, trying to find her voice, and finally succeeding. "This is outrageous! I'm not in league with the terrorists. I haven't been helping them. I was almost blown up and some of my best friends are dead, how can you even think I might be involved?"

"Cut the crap, Allison," Seles said. "No one else knew about the last two times that we were close, especially this last one, except you. Everyone is dead and now we're out of leads again. How convenient for you."

"It's not convenient for me!" she snapped. "If they knew you were coming it had nothing to do with me. Someone from one of your crew could have tipped someone off." Her face lit with fear as she paced around the room. Bolan stood silently with his arms crossed and waited for her to crack. A technician walked into the room with a stack of papers listing her phone log.

"We'll have her email archives in the next few minutes, sir," the technician said.

"You have no right to spy on me," Hart protested. "I'm not part of some conspiracy. The only person I've talked to all day is my boyfriend, but he'd be…"

She stopped in midsentence and Bolan could see the reality flooding down on top of her.

"That can't be… He would never…."

"Would that be Michael Jonas?" Bolan asked, scrolling through the call log. He noted the times of all of the calls and backtracked the last twenty-four hours in his head to see if they matched up. If she was working with someone on the outside it was literally *one* someone, as her call logs had only one number outside of her regular duty calls.

"Yes, but he's Director of Security at Ford Field! It was like sharing information with a police officer."

"Look at this," Bolan noted. "Two phone calls from Michael Jonas minutes before an operation was blown. Do you have his picture?"

"Yes." Hart pulled out her cell phone and scrolled through the pictures. She found one of just Michael and sent it to Bolan's phone. Bolan sent the picture to Brognola with a rush message for facial recognition.

"There has to be some other explanation," she muttered. "He can't have been using me this whole time. That would mean…all of this was my fault."

"There is no time right now for self-recrimination. I'm

sure your supervisors will be looking more deeply into this. Where was he when you spoke to him last?" Bolan asked.

"He was at the stadium. They have a packed house today for the game."

"Perfect soft target," Seles said.

Bolan's phone rang with Brognola on the other line.

"That was fast," Bolan said.

"Well, I was able to narrow it down with parameters from information we've gathered through the day. This is not Michael Jonas."

"Hold on. Let me put you on speaker and we can all work this out."

Bolan hit Speaker on his phone and set it in the middle of the table.

"Denny, Allison, I'll just introduce the voice on the other end of this phone as my eyes and ears."

"As I was saying, this is not Michael Jonas. The real Michael Jonas was killed and his identity stolen. This is Sayid Rais Sayf—he's on our terrorist watch list, but not someone we've been actively looking for. This isn't the first time we've heard his name today, and my guess is he's been orchestrating this whole thing. Born in Pakistan, educated in Europe, he then spent some time as a soldier before he went off the radar and was lost."

"Based on the information that we gained from the container and the traces that were left on the decoy can you estimate what damage we'd be looking at if he detonated this in the stadium?" Bolan asked.

"It depends on the nature of the weapon that he uses, but this guy is smart and I suspect he could decimate that stadium if he chose to do so."

"Agreed," Bolan said. "Thanks. We'll get back to you soon."

Bolan hung up the phone and stared at Hart, who'd turned

several shades whiter. There was no more incrimination and no more defense of her boyfriend. All other thoughts were replaced by a look of total devastation.

"We need to get to the stadium now," Bolan said.

Hart started to walk toward the door.

"Where do you think you're going?" Seles asked.

"I'll order the chopper. Be ready to leave in five minutes."

"You aren't coming with us," Seles said. "I'm still not sure that I trust you."

"Funny, after all of this, I'm not sure that I trust me, but I want to see this thing through to its end. After that I'll resign and they can do with me what they please, but for now I'm going to help bring this guy in."

The door closed and Seles turned to Bolan. "You think we should trust her?"

"I think she's the only one to trust right now. Did you see her face? She had no idea she was being used and there's no better weapon than a woman scorned."

"I hope you're right."

They raced to the helipad, hitting the armory on the way. Bolan, armed with his favorites, jumped on board the helicopter and took his place across from Hart. She looked out of place in a bulletproof vest, but he knew without saying a word that there would be no deterring her from the mission.

The ride in the helicopter seemed to take an eternity. Brognola had sent him the schematics for the field and Bolan scrolled through them to look for the points of vulnerability. Seles leaned over his shoulder as Bolan reviewed the plans. Bolan stopped at the junctions for the utilities and they noted the locations of the main structural beams.

Ford Field was packed and evacuation would take too long. Bolan prayed that they would be in time to disarm the bomb and not get anyone else killed. They circled the stadium one more time and finally found a place to land in the VIP parking lot. The dust from the rotor spun like a sandstorm around the expensive cars and limos, giving the once shiny parking lot a desert look.

They jumped out of the helicopter as it touched down and stayed ducked down until it lifted off the ground enough to stop kicking up debris. They made their way to the security entrance for the stadium.

"Are you ready for this?" Bolan asked Hart.

"No. I wasn't ready for any of it, but I'll finish the job."

22

Standing in the central security station, Sayf looked at his Rolex watch and shook his head. Yasim was either dead or in custody—he'd been gone almost an hour and hadn't called. Sayf's instincts told him that he was out of time and that if he didn't move to detonate the bomb, his entire plan would unravel. "I'm going to do a sweep," he said to the technicians at the monitors. "Let's keep our focus on the stands and concession areas."

"Yes, sir," one of the oblivious security guards replied, never taking his eyes off the screens in front of him.

Sayf slipped out of the station and headed down the hallway which would lead to the main thoroughfare corridors. By his estimation, it would take about ten minutes to get to the bomb, then another five for it to go off. Sayf wanted to be there when it did—to burn in the heart of the holy fire he'd worked so hard to bring down on this city. Anything less than that would be a failure in his mind.

His belt radio crackled and one of his security officers said, "Michael Jonas, do you copy?"

Sayf keyed the mike. "This is Jonas, go ahead."

"Sir, one of the owners just called and wants you to meet him in your office. Something about a problem in one of the luxury suites."

"Call him back and tell him I'll come to him," he said, having no intention of doing so.

"I can't, sir," the man replied. "He was on his way when he called."

Sayf considered it, then let out a frustrated sigh. He didn't want one of the owners poking around his office. He keyed the mike again. "All right. I'm on my way."

He reached the main concourse, following it around to the hallway that led to several offices, including his. Annoyed at the interruption, but unwilling to let an owner potentially spoil his plans, he yanked open the door and stepped inside.

Allison Hart was standing in front of his desk, her arms crossed. Two men, one on each side of her, stared at him coldly.

In an instant, Sayf knew that these were Cooper and Seles and that his cover had been completely blown. Still, he could play for time. "Allison," he said, taking a step toward her. "What an unexpected pleasure."

"I wish I could say the same, Michael. Or is it Sayid Rais Sayf?"

"Two totally different people," he replied, easing one of his hands behind his back and beneath his suit coat. "We all wear masks."

"Is that what you call it?" she snapped.

"Where's the bomb, Sayid?" the taller of the two men said. He was dark-haired, with broad shoulders and a narrow waist and a disturbingly direct gaze. Cooper, he decided.

"It doesn't matter now," he said. "You're too late to stop it."

"Bullshit!" the other man barked. "Tell us now, Sayid, or I'll take you down like the rabid dog you are."

"Rabid dog?" he said. "I am a warrior of Allah, and I will strike a mighty blow that will never be forgotten!" Sayf pulled his hand out from behind his back, revealing the gun he carried and firing it in one smooth motion.

In the relatively small confines of the office, it was fairly loud. He watched as their eyes widened in surprise, astonishment, and then Hart's blinked furiously in pain and understanding. The front of her shirt blossomed with blood.

The man called Cooper caught her as she fell, and Sayf turned and ran. They wouldn't give chase right away—not with the woman's life to save—and that would be all the time he needed to detonate the bomb.

"ALLISON, NO!" SELES SAID, whipping off his jacket and trying to staunch the flow of blood as Bolan lowered her to the floor. "Cooper, help me!"

"Listen, Denny, you have to take care of her. I've got to go after him," Bolan said.

Some light of reason came into Seles's eyes and he nodded. "I've got her. Go!"

Bolan leapt to his feet and raced out of the office. At the far end of the hallway, Sayf turned into the main concourse. Saving his breath, Bolan turned on the speed and hit the concourse at a full sprint.

The corridor was filled with people, making it hard to see, but the shouts of outrage and people yelling for someone to stop was all the trail he needed. He kept going, shouting, "Police officer, out of the way!" to force people to move.

He'd closed the gap substantially when two men in Ford Field security uniforms appeared out of the crowd. "Hold it, sir!" one of them shouted.

"Not now," Bolan snarled, barreling into him and knocking him to the ground. The other man jumped onto his back and Bolan was forced to pause. He spun to one side, flipping the man over his shoulder to land on the hard concrete of the concourse. "I'm a cop, you idiots," he said.

"We've been ordered to detain you," the first one said.

He couldn't have been a day older than twenty-one. "Now, if you'll come with us."

Sayf had deployed them to get free, Bolan knew, and every second counted. "Sorry, I can't," he said. He closed in and as the man tried to grab him, he slipped under his guard and delivered a hammer blow to his chest. Air whooshed out of his lungs and Bolan followed up with a sharp elbow to the temple. The man went down in a heap.

The second guard was struggling to rise as Bolan ran past him in the direction Sayf had gone. But with the concourse filled with milling people, it was hard to tell just where he might be headed. It was a huge stadium. Bolan spun on his heel and picked up the stunned security officer from the floor where he'd made it to his knees.

"Listen, kid," he said. "Does this stadium have a basement or a maintenance tunnel?"

"What?" he asked. "Yeah, sure. There's a whole basement substructure beneath the luxury boxes. It used to be an old warehouse or something."

"Which way?" Bolan asked.

The kid pointed down the concourse. "Take the…take the hallway marked M, and there's a set of stairs about halfway down that lead into the basement tunnels."

Bolan set him down. "Call your other security members and tell them to stand down." He didn't wait for a response, just turned and ran. It seemed to take forever to get through the crowd, but he made it to the hallway with a giant *M* painted over the top before he ran into another obstacle. These weren't security men, but two of Sayf's men.

They were closing fast and Bolan knew he didn't have time for a protracted fight. Gunfire might miss and hurt one of the innocent bystanders, or worse, cause a mass panic. He slipped into the hallway and waited, not wanting them running up behind him.

The two men came in ready for a fight, but Bolan struck fast and low. He lashed out with a kick that shattered the knee of the closest man, who screamed, then Bolan spun and drove an elbow into the nose of the other man, squashing it flat. The first man went to the ground, clutching his leg, but the second staggered away, shaking his head to clear his vision and then came forward at a full charge, bellowing like an enraged bull.

He hit Bolan square in the midsection, driving his legs like pistons, while the Executioner slammed blows into his back and neck. Once, twice, three times he hit him before the man finally slowed a bit. This was all Bolan needed as he wrapped his own strong arms around the man's neck and slipped behind him. He struggled wildly in Bolan's grasp, but wasn't fast enough. His neck broke with a resounding crack.

Bolan kept moving, and found the stairs leading down to the basement level. At the bottom, there was a locked door, but it was old and wooden, so two swift kicks shattered the wood around the lock and it swung open.

He dashed through and only his instinct for survival saved him as he caught sight of something out of the corner of his eyes and reacted, dodging for cover. The first barrage of bullets pinged and whined off the concrete and metal around him. If he'd been in the open, they would've cut him in half.

There were no bystanders down here, and the deep, low clank and thrum of the various HVAC and other machines would cover the noise of gunfire. He drew his Desert Eagle, wondering how many more men Sayf had down here. He suspected no more than two or three. If his group was much larger, it was likely that his plan would have unraveled much sooner. Keeping secrets, even among religious fanatics, isn't easy—and the larger the group, the harder it would be. Sayf wasn't stupid.

Peering around the space in the dim light, Bolan spotted

a large crescent wrench sitting atop one of the HVAC units. Picking it up, he hefted it in one hand and risked a quick glimpse into the narrow hallway. He didn't see anyone, but they were likely waiting for him to make a move.

He went down to one knee, then tossed the wrench as hard as he could with his left hand into an aluminum section of ductwork. The loud clang of its impact brought two men out from their hiding places, both of them shooting at once. Bolan fired without standing, putting two large slugs into the closest man, who screamed as the rounds penetrated his chest. He tumbled over backward, his desperate cries drawing the attention of the second man, who risked his own life to run to his fallen companion.

A mistake on his part. Bolan shot him down as he moved, the force of the slugs knocking him to the ground in a heap. Getting to his feet, the Executioner shoved the Desert Eagle back into its holster. He paused long enough to ensure that the two men were dead, then kept moving. The hallway narrowed, moving down until the concrete gave way to old brick.

He was truly in the bowels of the stadium, and there was little room to take cover if he was confronted. Ahead, he spotted a lighted room through an archway. He paused, and saw that Sayf was inside.

Kneeling on a prayer rug, he was mumbling to himself in his own language. In front of him in a metal frame was the bomb, and in his right hand, the device that would no doubt trigger the countdown. Bolan drew his gun once more, stepping into the room behind the terrorist.

"Don't move, Sayf," he said. "Don't even twitch."

"Do you think I fear you?" the man questioned, not turning around. "Do you think I fear death?"

"I don't give a damn what you fear," Bolan said. "But if you so much as take a breath I don't like, I'll kill you without a thought."

"You're too late," Sayf said, dropping the trigger. "Look at the timer."

Bolan peered over the terrorist's shoulder. The digital clock embedded in the faceplate read 4:28 and was counting down. "Shut it off," he ordered. "Now. It's over."

Sayf laughed softly, his shoulders jigging up and down as he tried to control himself. "I am the hand of Allah," he said. "I have succeeded where so many others have failed."

"Last chance," Bolan said.

"You won't kill me in cold blood," he said. "It is against your so-called laws." He laughed again. "Are you ready to die, American pig?"

"We have a saying in this country," Bolan growled. "It's not over until the fat lady sings." He squeezed the trigger on the Desert Eagle twice, and the weapon boomed like a cannon in the small space. The first round took Sayf in the right shoulder, the second in the left.

The bullets slammed him into the ground with a grunt and he hit his head on the old stone floor. Whether it was shock or the knock on the head, he was out like a proverbial light. Bolan knelt and tore Sayf's shirt off, then his own, using them as pressure bandages.

Turning his attention to the bomb, Bolan picked up the triggering device and began looking for a way to shut down the timer. Footsteps pounded down the hall and he turned, ready to fight, when Seles burst into the room.

"How'd you find me?" he asked.

"I just had to follow the trail of bodies to you," he quipped.

"Funny," Bolan said. "Do you know how to disarm this?"

"No, but maybe if we both hum along, we can fake it."

"Sounds like a plan," Bolan said. The two men began examining the bomb once more. The digital readout was down to just under three minutes.

"The triggering device won't be useful," Seles said. "We have to take the faceplate off and get to the detonator itself."

"Okay," Bolan said. There was a heavy tool kit on the floor next to the bomb that had probably been used to get the device in place. He opened it and took out a power screwdriver.

"Remove the screws around the timer," Seles said, "but don't touch any of the wires."

There were six screws holding the timer plate in place and Bolan went through them rapidly, then used the tip to pry the faceplate gently away from the bomb itself. "Got it," he said. "Ninety seconds."

Seles was looking at his handheld, then back at the bomb. "The configurations don't match with what I've got here," he said.

"Then *guess*," Bolan said.

"If you cut a wire, it could spark and set it off..." he mused. "And if you pull the power the same thing."

"And?"

"That's a bridge-wire detonator," Seles said. "Unscrew it from the housing. It can't fire without power. They've used it to make the circuit complete."

"Got it," Bolan said, reaching behind the timer and into the core of the device. The bridge detonator was a long, tube-shaped device that screwed down into the weapon. When fired, its charge would cause it to blow.

"Sixty seconds," Seles said.

Bolan began twisting it to the left, but it was incredibly slow going. The detonator was stiff and unyielding and the threads were tight against it.

"Forty-five."

"If you wouldn't mind," Bolan said, gritting his teeth and trying to go faster. Sweat beaded along his brow and his hand began to cramp from trying to twist the detonator in the tiny space.

"Thirty seconds, Cooper," Seles said.

Bolan felt the detonator give a little bit in his hand, then his grip slipped. "Damn it," he muttered. He refocused and tried again. This time it began to turn more freely.

"Twenty."

Bolan ignored him, trying to spin the detonator on the threads as fast as possible in the confined space. A high-pitched whine came from within the bomb itself as the power source they'd used began to cycle up to a higher voltage. Considering how he was situated, a massive electrical shock wasn't out of the question.

"Ten," Seles said.

"Almost there," Bolan grunted, spinning it faster. It was almost free.

"Five, four, three…"

The detonator slipped free and Bolan yanked it out of the bomb. The power source finished its cycle and the timer reached zero, a loud beeping sound coming from the housing. The charge fired, but without a detonator to complete the connection, it passed harmlessly into the metal sphere and dissipated.

"Thin," Bolan said, holding the detonator in his hand. "Mighty thin."

A huge roar shook the building from the fans upstairs.

"I'm thinking touchdown," Seles replied, grinning.

"Yeah, me, too," Bolan said. "Me, too."

Epilogue

"What's next for you?" Seles asked as Bolan watched Sayf being taken to an ambulance under heavy guard. It looked like the man would live, but there was no way he'd ever be free again.

"Next?" Bolan replied. "I'm not sure."

"What about your drug case?"

"I think this solved it. My guess is that Sayid was using the money to get his hands on the materials he needed to build his weapon. Besides, things will be very quiet here for a while."

"You aren't really a DEA agent," Seles said. "And you're not any kind of regular law enforcement. Walker figured that out. Who are you really?"

Bolan shrugged into the T-shirt someone had brought him from the concession area, then put his shoulder holster and jacket back on. "Matt Cooper," he said. "That's all I can tell you."

Seles laughed. "You either can't or won't say, will you?"

Bolan held out a hand and they shook. "I'm sorry that Allison was killed," he said. "And the others. I wish I could've done more."

"You did enough. We couldn't have stopped them without you."

"It was good working with you, Special Agent in Charge

Denny Seles. Do you think they'll promote you when all this is said and done and the paper trail made invisible?"

"It's possible," he replied. "But I'm happy here. This is my town."

"Then I'm glad you got to keep it in one, relatively whole, piece."

"Me, too, Cooper. When can I expect your report on all this?"

Bolan laughed and clapped Seles on the shoulder, then started walking toward the SUV. "Yeah, well, I'm not so good with the paperwork part, but I know you can handle it."

"Cooper! I mean it! I'll need your full statement to include."

The big man ignored him, tossing a wave over his shoulder before he got into his vehicle. "Cooper! Don't leave me with all the paperwork!"

The SUV's window rolled down and Bolan smiled at him. "I wouldn't do that to you, would I?" he asked. "I have a feeling that the paperwork will work itself out." Before Seles could respond, the window went back up and the SUV rolled away.

* * * * *